SINGLE DAD plus one

By JJ Knight

Copyright © 2017 by JJ Knight. All rights reserved.

No part of this book may be used or reproduced by any means, graphic, electronic, or mechanical, including photocopying, taping, and recording without written permission.

All the characters, organizations, and events portrayed in this novel are either products of the author's imagination or used fictitiously.

FIRST EDITION
ISBN: 978-1977566584

Also by JJ Knight

The UNCAGED LOVE Series
The FIGHT FOR HER Series

www.jjknight.com

For all the single daddies

Chapter 1: Dell

I love women.

The luscious sensation of holding them in my arms.

The downy softness of their skin.

The smell of baby poo —

Wait.

I shake myself awake.

I've fallen asleep in the rocking chair again, baby Grace on my chest.

And I feel —

Uggh. Sticky.

I shift positions and Grace's head pops up. She

gives me a huge baby girl grin.

Yeah, I bet you feel great.

I try to stand up from the rocking chair, but I sense something oozing down my bare chest. Yeah, it's sliding.

Shoot. If I move, I'm going to get baby sludge all over the rocking chair cushions, the rug, everywhere.

Why the hell did I get a penthouse this big? Where is my butler?

Not that he'd help.

He has a no-baby clause in his contract.

I glance at the clock. It's 2 a.m. Arianna's undoubtedly sound asleep in the master bedroom way down the hall. It's her work day tomorrow, so I had the night duty.

I'm on my own.

The room is dim, lit only by a night-light. I need something that is easy to throw in the wash to catch this disaster that has blown out the baby's diaper and leaked through her sleeper.

I spot a burp cloth tossed over the edge of the crib. Perfect. If I lean far enough, I can probably reach it.

I hold Grace in place. Her head has thunked back

down on my chest, but she's wiggly. Not sleeping. I don't want her to get too riled up. If she starts kicking and fussing, the shit will literally fly.

My right arm reaches, extending across the space between the rocking chair and the crib. I lean, keeping Grace firmly in place on my chest.

I almost graze it. The cotton brushes my fingers.

Just a little farther. I've almost got it.

I feel the rocker start to tilt. Then the unsettling sensation of an unexpected shift in weight as the glider mechanism slides forward.

"Whoa!" I cry, pulling my arm back and trying to right the chair.

But we've gone too far, and I curl my arms around Grace as it crashes over.

I roll out of it, my body around the baby. She laughs like we're on an amusement park ride.

The chair makes a terrible racket, the arm hitting the hardwood floor just past the rug and the back tangling into the slats of the crib.

I take the brunt of the fall with my elbow and recover rather gracefully, I must say, getting right back to my feet after completing a full roll.

Grace giggles, her little legs kicking with

excitement.

But I can feel it. Goop. Everywhere.

And footsteps down the hall, hurried.

Great.

Arianna arrives, flipping on the light. "Is everything all right?"

The baby monitor in our bedroom amplifies noise in the nursery. It probably sounded like the building was collapsing.

"Just knocked the rocking chair over," I say, blinking in the brightness. Her honeyed curls are mashed on one side, a robe thrown over a tank top and sleep shorts.

"Are you okay?" Her eyes frantically search me, then Grace, one hand shielding her eyes so she can see in the light. Then she waves her hand in front of her nose.

"Oh, God, Dell! What in the world?"

In the brightness of the overhead, the destruction is impressive. The chair, leaning into the crib. Cushions on the floor. And the smears. Yellow-green poop. On the arm of the rocker. On the floor where we landed, a spray from the impact of the fall.

And all down my body, my belly, my shorts.

"Too many peas, maybe?" I say.

"Too much something."

Adding solids to Grace's diet has been an experience.

Bernard arrives, as put together as he can be for the hour in hastily donned black pants and a button-up shirt. "Is everything all right, sir?"

Then he sees the room, the floor, and me. "I'll call the housekeeper," he says, backing from the room.

"No, no," Arianna says. "It's the middle of the night. We'll handle it."

"I'll fetch a bucket, then," he says, his lips pressed together.

"Poor Bernard," she says and turns back to me. "I'd take the baby, but um, no."

The next visitor is Maximillion, my greyhound. He hurtles into the room like he's going to save the day, all muscle and lean legs.

Then he halts.

His nose sniffs the air, uncertain, interested.

Then he looks at me as if to say, "Hell, no."

And bounds back down the hall.

I glance over at Arianna.

"Even the dog deserted us."

She laughs. "I don't blame him."

I hold Grace up in the air. She giggles, her legs working. She's wet and gooey from the waist down, the pink sleeper soaked to orange.

"I can't believe she isn't fussing in that mess," Arianna says.

"Can you turn on the shower?" I ask her. "I think I'll just take us both in."

"Sounds like a good idea," she says. "I'll take care of this out here."

"I can get it. It's my mess," I say.

"No," she says. "It's our mess. Our perfect, precious mess." She surveys the room. "Did you jump up or squeeze her when she blew out the diaper?"

"Something like that," I say.

She shakes her head. "Let me get the water on."

I follow her, holding Grace out and away from my body.

Grace loves flying, and her arms and legs wiggle like crazy, her face lit up with happiness. Despite the hour, the poop explosion, and the disgust of my butler, I count this one as a good memory.

"All ready," Arianna says, stepping back from the

shower. Her nose wrinkles as she looks at us. "I'd offer to pull your shorts down, but I'm not sure I want to touch them."

"I don't think I've ever failed a proposition in quite this way," I say with a chuckle. "We're going in fully dressed to get the worst off."

"Okay," she says. "You can hand me the clothes."

I pull Grace close and step into the spray.

Grace squints her eyes, arms waving, not sure what to think of the water. I lift her up, letting the flow rinse the worst of the mess from her sleeper. Then I move her out of the way so it can hit me as well.

"Is she okay in there?" Arianna asks.

"She seems to be perplexed by the whole experience," I say.

"She's not crying."

"She seems more curious than anything."

And she is. Grace looks down on me and the water, fascinated.

I turn my back to the spray. "All right, little one, let's get you stripped down."

The snaps are tricky with the wet fabric sticking

to her. I cradle her in one arm and work them with the free hand. Finally I'm able to peel it away.

"First one," I say, passing it outside the curtain.

Arianna takes it from me.

The diaper is huge and puffy. I pull it off, rolling it up the best I can before holding it out. "Big bomb incoming," I say.

"Yuck," she says. "Just drop it."

I peek around the curtain. Arianna holds a plastic bag out, ready to catch it.

That taken care of, I turn Grace back into the water, careful to keep her face from getting pummeled too hard by the spray. She loves it, reaching out to catch the streams, feet kicking.

"You ready for a clean baby?" I call out.

"Just a sec," Arianna says.

We play in the spray a little longer. My boxers are sticking to me, and I long to get them off and be done with this.

The curtain slides a few inches. "Okay, I'll take her now."

I pass Grace to Arianna and peel out of the shorts. Arianna pauses to watch a moment, making my cock stir despite our predicament.

She holds out her hand.

"You wanting some of this?" I ask her with a laugh.

"Just the wet shorts, mister," she says. "The rest can wait."

"Is that a promise?" I hold on to the boxers.

Now she cracks a smile. "Of course it is."

I hand her the sodden fabric. "Be out in a second."

What a night. I quickly soap down, sighing to be free of the mess. Fatherhood. I certainly hadn't seen this day coming. But in the months since we got Grace, I've learned that everything I thought to be true about how I wanted to live my life was wrong.

Arianna is a treasure. Grace is a joy. I'm working part-time and it's been just fine. We've found our own way to be a family. Even in the bizarre moments like this, we are content.

There's just one problem left to handle. When I think about it, my hand tightens on the washcloth, wringing it out.

Arianna and I are engaged, and she wants to meet my parents.

But I haven't told them about her. Or Grace.

They don't know I've changed my name.
They know nothing about me.
And eventually I will have to face it all.

Chapter 2: Arianna

Morning comes more quickly than I'd like after our middle-of-the-night cleanup. Dell sleeps soundly, one arm thrown across his forehead.

I slide my phone from beneath my pillow, where it quietly buzzes an alarm. I shut it off and pause, listening to the baby monitor. Silence there too.

Good. I pad to the shower to begin my day. I have two new hires for the fall, and I need to watch them closely. Del Gato Child Spa is all about nurturing the children in its care, and I must carefully assess anyone coming on board. It takes a certain type of person to hold her ground both firmly and kindly in the face of a roomful of two-year-olds.

As I shampoo my crazy curls, still wishing for something that would take the frizz away without time-consuming blowouts, I try to remember a time my own mother had to handle misbehavior.

Our days together were rare. I can recall some breakfasts, me at a table with the cook while my parents raced around. And a few bedtimes, when one or the other would pop in to kiss me, usually bedecked in a glittery dress or crisp tux.

They always left the room smelling of jasmine or woodsy cologne. I still associate those smells with adventure and excitement. The life my parents led without me.

I'm not making that same mistake. And my Child Spa helps lessen the blow to other children whose parents are as busy as mine were.

When I step out of the bathroom in my robe, Dell has vacated the bed. I lean over to the baby monitor to see if he's in the nursery.

He is. He's talking to Grace in his usual way, all "Good morning" and "Should we review today's financial news?"

He makes me laugh. We're careful to find a

balance between our careers and our daughter. We're there for breakfast *and* bedtime, both of us whenever possible. We have routines and lullabies, and lots and lots of love.

I'm glad at least one of us was raised normally. Dell had a mother and father who lived with him all the time, not between international meetings.

I head into the closet, revamped so that both Dell and I can share the space. It's more cramped than it was before, and more chaotic than Bernard likes. But it works.

As if to remind myself that Dell is a normal guy with regular parents, I open his Alabama drawer. Everything is how I remember it. The Auburn sweatshirt. The Birmingham Bulls hat.

Nestled inside is the clock that helped me put together the clues to his hidden past. That crazy man decided his background mucking the kennels at a greyhound racetrack was unbecoming of the man he wanted to be. At age twenty-three, he changed his name and purged anything he could from the Internet.

But I know who he is.

Just not really who he *was*.

I hold up my hand, shifting the engagement ring

in the light. Dell talks to his mother occasionally, this I do know. I assume he's told her about me.

But I'm not really sure.

Last week I decided to press the issue and ask to meet them. We've been together four months now. The holidays are approaching and I need to be able to tell my parents if I'll see them or if I'll be in Alabama.

Of course, I haven't told my parents about our engagement either.

We've kept things a secret. I don't wear my ring at work.

The public is more or less ignorant. Dell was a favorite in the society press as a bachelor, but as a settled man, not so much. So nobody's spying.

Even if they were, Dell and I haven't really had time for charity balls or big public events. Grace is a handful and we like being there for her, not surrounded by socialites and hounded by photographers.

Early on, there was a big rush to figure out who the baby was. We told a few key gossips that I was a single mom, and that settled it. I was too boring to pursue for long, plain-Jane me with my frizzy hair, small business, and lackluster history.

Until yesterday, when I visited the DOMs at a bar and spilled the beans, nobody knew Dell had proposed.

God, the DOMs. The Dirty Old Mistresses. They'd kicked me right out, as their group was only for Dell's exes. But I got a definite undercurrent of displeasure, as if frumpy ol' me landing one of their eligible bachelor billionaires was an affront to their sensibilities.

I like our story being a secret. It keeps things easy. The adoption is well underway. It should be complete as soon as the French side of things is taken care of. Even Dell's influence hasn't been able to speed up the paperwork on that side.

But Grace's mother is the ultimate secret. The Duchess has given Grace to us to raise. The DNA test bore out that Dell was indeed the father. All that has been left is for me to become her mother. We've already decided to elope if needed to hurry things along.

I don't need a big society wedding.

Do I?

Dang, now I'm late. I shove Dell's drawer closed and snatch the closest dress, a lovely wraparound green number that makes my boobs look smashing. Dell's eyes never fail to get mesmerized by them when I wear it.

I toss a pair of chocolate wedge heels on the floor and slide my feet inside. Then I snatch a pair of emerald earrings as I pass the jewelry tray. Within minutes, I've hurried down the hall to eat a quick bite before I have to rush downstairs to the Child Spa.

Dell is in the breakfast nook, spooning oatmeal into Grace in her high chair. She's wearing one of the samples from the baby wear line he bought. It's a red velour jumper dress that reads "Got Math?"

As expected, his gaze gravitates to my cleavage and lingers on the swells. I lean over to kiss Grace on her fuzzy pale head, knowing I've just added more boob fuel to the fire.

He clears his throat. "So, she takes a nap at eleven if you can get away."

This makes me smile. It's true that on my work days, I do sometimes take a break and visit him. It's just a forty-floor ride that separates us, since my Child Spa is in the same building.

A glance at his workout shorts tells me he's more than a little anxious for my return.

"I'll try to slip away," I say.

Bernard enters with a plate of fluffy egg whites and sizzling bacon. I sit down to eat them, watching Dell's attempts to spoon oatmeal into Grace. Most of it ends up on her bib and face.

He has an empty cereal bowl. I tilt my head toward it. "You didn't eat the last of the Cap'n Crunch, now, did you?" I ask.

Bernard reappears with a box. "I would not allow that to happen."

"Uggh, that's the one without berries," I say, wrinkling my nose.

He looks at it. "My apologies. Would you like a bowl with berries?" His sneer on the word *berries* suggests that it's an affront to call the dyed puffs of sugar the same name as a healthy fruit.

It's an old joke around here already.

"Not today," I say. "I'm late." I swallow another bite of eggs, pick up the last piece of bacon, and lean in for a kiss from Dell. "Can't miss the morning drop-offs!"

Grace waves her arms and gurgles happily. I kiss her again too. "Work on that army crawl, darling," I say to her. She's just started to figure out how to scoot across the floor with her elbows. She'll be big-time on the move soon.

"I'll text you when she's asleep," Dell says, eyebrow lifted.

I shoot him a knowing smile.

Life is good to us.

Chapter 3: Dell

After Arianna's off, I give up on cereal for Grace and pull her out of the high chair. Bernard arrives to whisk the mess away, and I remove her bib and take her with me to the study.

She's pretty good about playing in this bouncy contraption with a dozen buttons and buzzers while I do a quick look through the business news of the day. If she fusses, I can generally get away with holding her in my lap and reading the article summaries out loud. If I use the Goofy voice while I do it, she'll giggle all the way through the *Wall Street Journal* headlines.

But when I set her down and power up my

computer, a notification pops up to call my mother. A quick glance at the calendar confirms that it's been fourteen days since I spoke with her. She keeps track.

I would prefer to wait until tomorrow, when I'm at work and Grace isn't there to potentially alert my mother to her existence. I know it's shameful that I've kept both the baby and Arianna a secret. But I'm not ready. She'll want me to come visit, and then there's the issue of privacy, and how I'll explain all this, and not to mention the worst of all.

My father.

My hand stills over the cell phone charging on my desk. I don't want Grace to know him. At all. I won't have him saying one negative thing to her, ever. I'm not sure I can control myself if he does. A lifetime of resentment might bubble over.

Still, it's her day. If I don't call her by lunchtime, she will call me. And the situation might not be as good then as it is now.

I glance over at Grace. She's happily banging the nose of a clown face that says, "A ha ha" over and over again. I taped over the speakers the first day it arrived to muffle the noise. Otherwise I'd have pitched it off the balcony within an hour.

Our conversations are never long. Mom has zero patience for long talks. Grace will be fine.

I should do it.

The phone is warm from the charger. I pick out my mother's number from the line of previous calls, the same ten digits from my childhood. The call rings. I can picture the beige cordless on the kitchen wall. Maybe she's upgraded since then. I haven't actually ventured home in well over ten years. Thirteen, in fact.

"Hello?" My mother's voice always startles me, gravelly and low. She's getting older. I should do better about seeing her.

"It's me, Mom," I say. "Is this a good time?"

"Better now than never," she says. "How is life in the big city?"

"Same as always." I glance over at Grace. She's sliding colored beads on a metal loop.

"You sound different. What's up?"

I can picture her in jeans and a T-shirt with the arms cut out, probably sitting on the counter with a cigarette in her hand. That's another strike. She can't smoke around this baby.

"Just work things. You know, the old grind."

"Your brother is here this week. It's too bad you can't come too. He's all grown up. Twenty-three and ready to take on the world."

Donovan. He was the winner in the name game. He could go by Don. Donny. Van. I'd had to change mine completely. I haven't seen him since he was a kid, although I'd quietly arranged for a full scholarship for him to go to college.

"What's he up to?" I ask.

"He finished his diploma, degree, whatever. You missed his graduation."

"I know. I'm sorry."

"He's been looking for a job all summer. Finally landed something and thought he'd spend his last free week with his family. Some children do that, you know."

I accept the admonishment. "What's he going to do?" Donovan was always a jokester, never taking anything seriously. I'm honestly surprised he made it through college at all.

"Got some job in some office," she says. "Pushing damn papers around. Like you, I guess. Fancy pants."

My parents are blue collar to the core. They don't

trust office work. And they have no idea I've changed my name. No one does, other than Arianna and a law firm that handled the legal paperwork. There is no connection between my former life and my current one.

Visiting them is a bit of a liability. They will call me Hasmund McDonald. I can't imagine having any associates in Birmingham, but if one spotted me, they would call me Dell. It's part of the reason I haven't gone back.

But now Arianna is pushing the issue. And my mother. Maybe I can control the situation. Avoid my hometown by luring them elsewhere.

"Have you given any more thought to a little trip, maybe with Donovan?" I ask her. "To celebrate his graduation?"

"Oh, we had a cake," she says. "Marge made it."

"But a trip would be great for him. See a little of the world before he goes. Maybe Italy or France."

"Hardly. It's damn far and your father simply can't leave the track for that long."

"He wasn't invited."

I can picture her rolling her eyes. "Hasmund, you've got to stop the pissy kid act. He was a great father. Look how you turned out."

Despite him, I think. "I wish you'd change your mind about a trip."

"It wouldn't hurt you to come down here. We could have dinner up at the VA Hall. They have a pancake supper every third Saturday. Two-dollar well drinks."

Breakfast and booze. That's my mother.

I take a deep breath. Maybe it's time to mention Arianna at least. Be vague about the timeline of our relationship. I'll have to fudge Grace's background.

"Mom, I've met a nice woman."

"Well, hell!" she cries. "I knew it! I told Beatrice next door that you had to have a girl in your life. It's in your voice."

My voice? I clear my throat. "We've been together quite a while. And, well, we've decided to get married."

Another screech. Then, from the depths of the house, "What in the world, woman?"

My father.

Mom calls out to him, "It's Hasmund. He's getting married!"

I can't hear his response. My throat tightens. I

turn to Grace, who looks like she might be getting bored with her toy. She's stopped playing and squirms in the seat, pushing with her arms as if to lift herself out. She might fuss any second.

"So if you'd like to come up, I'd be happy to introduce you to her," I say.

"You have to bring her here!" she says. "You have to! Aunt Marge and Uncle Travis will want to meet her. And your great-aunt Ethel and the twins and everyone from the track. Johnny is still there, you know, and Becky and Jeremy."

"We are *not* going to visit the track," I say firmly. God, that would be a disaster. Thirteen years of eradicating my past, undone in one moment.

"But Hasmund, this is a big deal," Mom says. "Nobody ever thought you were going to settle down. You know, Barb just had her fourth kid. And Beatrice is a grandmother three times over."

It's on the tip of my tongue to tell her she is one too, but I stop myself. I have close to eighteen months to explain once I bring up Grace, and Arianna and I have not come up with a proper cover story.

Mom's voice has taken on a younger, girlish quality. "I'm going to have Marge make one of her double chocolate fudge cakes for this. Extra big. Nothing is too good for my boy. Married! Do you have a date? Are you going to do it here at the VA? Becky did it there and they used a bunch of candles and it looked real classy."

I bet it did.

"We haven't gotten that far," I tell her. "I'm sure Arianna will want to plan things."

"Arianna," Mom says. "Love it. Sounds like a real down-home girl. I can't wait. Can't you come before Donovan is gone? I'll set up the air mattress. If we move the sofa against the back wall, there's enough room for it. Of course you and Donovan can sleep on your bunks in your old room. I was thinking for your lady."

I picture Arianna sleeping between the TV console and the ragged sofa on an air mattress and try to figure out how to explain to my mother that this isn't who I am anymore.

"I don't really want to be around Dad," I say. "I'm not going to budge on that."

"Well, damn," she says. "I can't exactly kick him out of his own house."

"You sure I can't convince you to meet me

somewhere? It can be close. Maybe a nice cruise? We can take one right out of Mobile."

I can hire a private boat, easy.

"Now, Hasmund McDonald, I've told you I'm not going to leave your father just because you're being irrational."

I sigh. "Okay, Mom."

Grace has started screwing up her face. Before she can make a sound, I pick her up, flying her through the air, the phone pressed between my cheek and shoulder.

"I should go," I say. Grace will giggle if I do anything too fun. Cry if I stop. A bead of sweat slides down my brow. My time is up. "I have to work."

"All right," she says. "Donovan is here until Sunday. I expect you to come down."

"I'll talk to Arianna about it," I say.

"She better say yes if I'm going to like her," she says.

"That's ridiculous, Mom," I say.

"So is not visiting for thirteen years!"

She's got me there. "All right. Talk soon."

I bring Grace down and kill the call just before the first fussy cry.

That was close.

But now I have a real dilemma. My mother expects me in a big way. Arianna wants to meet her and I don't want everybody to start off on the wrong foot.

But I don't see how I can go to Alabama with an eight-month-old baby and a four-month-old relationship.

Chapter 4: Arianna

I admit that even four months in, I still think about Dell — a lot — when I'm down in the Child Spa, especially if I'm feeling restless.

The place hums along, only a couple small details to attend to other than the usual routine. Everyone seems happy to see me, both the teachers and the children. It may help that I'm not here every day.

Going part-time was a good change.

I check the clock as I walk by. Just past eleven. Close enough to pass for lunchtime. I quickly text Dell.

Is the baby sleeping?

A little zing zips through me. Even though I'm marrying Dell and know him better than anybody, it's still a thrill to proposition him in the middle of the day.

My phone buzzes.

She's down.

I hustle along the hall to the back exit to the elevators and send another text.

Be naked.

His response is swift.

I plan to. Will you?

Another charge bolts through me. That man.

I step into the elevator and hold the card key up to the sensor that will let me up to the penthouse. This will alert Bernard, the butler, that I'm coming up. Given the hour, he will probably be preparing lunch.

Do I dare get naked before I go up there?

Dell has asked. The doors close and I'm alone in the elevator. I glance up at the camera in the corner. I can't do it here.

But then I get another text. I glance down at the phone in my hand.

Get busy. I'm watching.

I text back. *Can't the guards see?*

I cut the feed to our elevator months ago. I'm the only one who can activate the camera.

I remember him mentioning this now. Plus, he's too protective of me to let some random guards watch me undress.

I'm waiting.

I look up at the camera. Dell leaves nothing to chance. I'm sure only he can see.

I kick off my shoes. Today's dress is all one piece. It wraps around and ties at the waist. I pull on the string.

My phone buzzes.

That's what I'm talking about.

A strong shot of desire bolts through me as the dress falls open. I shrug my shoulders and let it drop to the floor of the elevator. It's moving now, slowly making its ascent.

My phone vibrates again.

Breasts. I must see them.

I shake my head with a smile and reach behind my back for the hooks of the bra. It isn't easy with the phone in my hand, but I manage.

I look up at the camera, feeling shy for a moment.

A text.

Please. I can't take it.

I drop my arms and let the bra slide to the floor.

Jesus.

We're almost to the top. I slide the lace panties down. I'm nervous now. What if the housekeeper is in the penthouse and decides to leave? Is there a delivery person in the private hall?

I step out of the panties. The elevator glides to a stop.

But the doors don't open.

I glance at the panel. A red button is lit up.

Emergency override.

What has he done? I'm about to text him when he sends a message.

Lift those beautiful breasts for me.

I'm caught between anxiety and desire, fear of being found and the intoxicating idea of being watched and instructed.

I set the phone on the floor in front of me and place my hands beneath my heavy breasts and lift them.

The phone lights up so I glance down at it.

Touch those nipples.

Good lord. A rush of heat rolls through me, but I do as he asks, rolling both nipples between my thumb and finger.

My breathing is harder now.

Legs a little farther apart.

I do that.

Lean back against the wall.

I take a step back. I'm lost now, forgetting anything that might disrupt the heat of this moment. Dell and I get a little wild sometimes, but we've never done anything like this.

Spread the folds.

I release one of my breasts and reach down.

The phone lights up again.

Beautiful. Now feel how slick you are.

I close my eyes and obey.

This is why things never get old with Dell, why he doesn't stray. We get crazy, do incredible risky things.

Hold right there.

I do, taking in the elevator, the gentle whir of the air vent above me, a slight whiff of cleaner. I wonder if anyone is sitting outside the elevator bank on the lower floors, wondering why one of the cars is stuck at the top. This is the only one that goes all the way to the penthouse.

The doors slide open.

My eyes fly wide, but it's him, of course it is, naked as he promised.

His chest is smooth and strong, muscles cutting across his pecs and shoulders.

When he speaks, his voice is low. "Spread wider."

I do, and he kneels in front of me. His mouth falls against my tender folds, tongue inside me.

I gasp and hold on to the rails, steadying my back against the cool walls of the elevator. He takes my leg and slides my thigh over his shoulder, diving in more deeply.

It's too much, the titillation of stripping for him in the public space, his commands, the way he made me touch myself.

And now, his mouth and hands and head. His hair tickles my belly. My hips roll with his movements. We move together like one person.

The intensity begins to build. I need him to work harder, faster. I grind against him, anxious, desperate.

He takes me to the edge, that precipice of no return, then he quickly pulls away, turning me around to face away.

I grab on to the rails as he slides powerfully into my body. His arms come around me, one holding on to my ribs. The other slips down, his fingers working me again.

I'm so far gone already that my body splinters right away, shuddering with sensation, the orgasm flooding out from where we join.

Behind me, Dell loses his controlled even strokes and crashes into me, his body strong and bold as he unleashes.

My hands grasp the rails, my breathing ragged. Dell holds on to me a little longer, letting both of us find our bearings. The base of the elevator isn't like a normal floor. You can sense it shifting on its rails, the slight give.

He withdraws and turns me around to hold me tightly against his chest. I feel both drained and exhilarated at the same time. Just like Dell to turn me inside out on my lunch break.

"I suppose we should return the elevator back to its normal use," he says. He bends down to pick up my clothes. He types a code into the elevator panel and the doors slide open. The red emergency button goes out.

I snatch up my phone and follow him into the private hall. "I should probably dress out here before Bernard gets an eyeful," I say.

Dell shrugs. "He's busy in the kitchen. He knows by now not to approach me when I'm not dressed, lest he see more of my activities than he prefers."

Still, I take my dress from Dell and drag it around my shoulders as we head through the front door. We stop by the open nursery door to check on Grace. She's still asleep in her crib, one arm over her head.

"Forget the elevator," I say. "The big risk was having her wake up with only Bernard in the penthouse."

Bernard does not do babies.

"I know her pretty well," Dell says. "She isn't waking up for a half hour yet."

We move on back to the master bedroom. Only when I get there and go through the things Dell spills onto the bed do I realize something is missing.

My panties were left on the floor of the elevator and are heading downstairs without me.

Chapter 5: Dell

After Arianna returns to her work, the subject of my mother and my visiting brother weighs on me. I didn't bring it up to her, not yet. I need to think some things through.

I plow through the crowd outside a bus stop near Central Park, Grace strapped to my back. It's a ticking clock, this visit she wants with the rest of the family all together. Perhaps for the last time. I have until Sunday.

But there are holidays. Thanksgiving. Christmas. I could wait.

But do I want my father destroying those special

days for us? They will be the first together for me and Arianna.

Damn.

We break free of the mass of people and my pulse slows down as we walk along the familiar hills and paths of the park.

When we approach a playscape, I reach behind to release a strap and swing Grace around to my front.

She lets out her baby giggle, waving her arms in a red jacket. She has a smart little knit hat on her head with two pink fuzzy ears that stick up. I can't imagine my life without her now.

We head for an open baby swing, the little bucket kind with holes where their feet fit through. I would never have figured the contraption out if it hadn't been for watching other parents stuff their wiggly offspring into them.

So much of parenting goes on behind closed doors. You can only see the way a family projects itself publicly. And that is no good. Arianna has much more experience in these matters than I do, but we still find gaps in our knowledge. How do you know if you are spoiling them? Can they really be spoiled? Isn't that just nurturing?

I have no answers.

Grace recognizes the swing and stills her kicking. She's smart, this one. She slides in easily, and I give her a gentle push.

See, another parenting dilemma. Do you literally push them to their limit, helping them get braver and stronger? Or do you keep it easy, keeping the swing at an easy pace that gives them no concern?

Damned if I know. It will only get more confounding as she grows.

This brings me full circle back to the issue of my family. Don't they deserve to know her, and her them? She'll find my younger brother silly and fun. My mother will dote on her.

But there's the issue of my father. His negativity. His hate.

Damned if I don't know a blessed thing.

"What do you think, Grace?" I ask. "Should we go see your grandmother?"

She waves her baby arms and lets out a cackle.

"Right, who wouldn't love you?"

I sincerely wish I could convince my mother to meet me anywhere but Birmingham. I can't be dragged to the racetrack.

And Arianna is not sleeping on an air mattress on the floor.

I give Grace another push and flick my phone to dial my office.

"Geneva? Dell. Look at five-star hotels in Birmingham, Alabama. Arrange the full transportation package, but not flashy on the car. I'll take my own plane."

My assistant is used to conversations like this. "When will you leave?" she asks.

Hell, I don't know.

"Assume Friday but let me get back to you."

"Return date?"

"Uh, I'll get back to you on that too."

Indecision *isn't* what she's used to. "Is everything all right, Mr. Brant?"

"Perfect. Just a family thing. Find hotels, a car, a driver." Maybe that's too much. "Scratch the driver." I hesitate. "No, actually, book one but let the service know I might not use him. I'll pay his rate either way."

Geneva hesitates, then says, "Are you sure you're okay?"

"It's complicated," I say. Since when did she get so personal?

But I know. I look over at Grace. Since the news got out about the baby. Other than a few key people at the Child Spa, everyone thinks she belongs to Arianna and I'm playing stepdad. We haven't corrected them. The secret of Grace's mother is too important.

"I'll get this arranged," she says, her tone back to professional. "Let me know the dates at your convenience."

"Thanks."

Grace starts fussing in the swing, so I pull her out. "You want to go visit Mommy?" I ask her. "We'll see what she thinks about Alabama."

I don't bother strapping Grace in, carrying her on my arm back through the park. We pass hot dog stands and two musicians. Grace's eyes light up when she hears a fiddle, so we stop and listen. She waves her arms and her joy is enough for me to fund this guy for a while, dropping most of my cash in his case.

It only takes fifteen minutes to get out of the park and cut through the building to the front side and the entrance to Arianna's Child Spa. When we push through the doors, Taylor stands up from behind her desk, holding out her arms.

"Let me see that squishy little love bug!" she says.

I hand her over, glancing around the foyer. Arianna is revamping the space to spotlight some of the best pieces of the children's clothing line I bought. The coffee shop next door has its lease up in six months, and I'm watching them closely to see if they will renew. If not, we might expand and add a curated children's shop that connects to the Child Spa.

Otherwise, the space still holds fond memories of the first time I met her, dragging in a baby carriage and a foul-smelling Grace.

Arianna comes through the locked gateway to the children's rooms. "Dell, what a surprise! Is everything okay?" She glances anxiously around until she spots Grace in Taylor's arms.

"Yeah," I say. "Taylor, can you watch her for a sec?"

"Sure!" she says, smashing the baby's cheek against hers. "Can't I, love bug?"

I shake my head. Thank goodness I read the newspaper to her to balance out the baby talk.

Arianna leads us back through the spa hallways to her office. "What's up?" she asks. "You need to go in today after all?"

"No," I say. "I'm trying to figure out a way to see my mother without my father, but she's being stubborn."

Arianna slides into her chair behind her desk. She's still wearing the green dress she stripped off in the elevator earlier today, and I remind myself to cool my jets as I drop into a chair opposite her.

But her face lights up. "Are we going to see her finally? With Grace?"

I rub my eyes. "I don't know. My brother is there until the end of the week. He's starting a new job. She wants us to come down." I don't mention that the "us" is just her, so far.

Arianna stands up, walking around her office as if she can't think well if she's sitting. "I could postpone a few things. Did you want to go the whole week? Or just the weekend?"

"Oh, I don't think I can manage more than two days with them," I say. "But we haven't thought through this baby thing."

She pauses in front of a bookcase and turns. "What do you mean?"

"Well, the whole world has bought the cover story that Grace is yours and I just walked into the picture. Do we try that number with my family?"

"How discreet are they?" she asks.

"Oh, somewhere between a parrot and the *National Enquirer.*"

She sinks back onto her chair. "I guess we'll have to keep the ruse, then. We can't afford anyone figuring out the truth."

"I know."

We sit a moment, our eyes locked, realizing the predicament we're in. We don't want to lie to everyone, but I don't see a choice.

"What were you going to tell your parents?" I ask her. "We've never hashed this out."

"They can be trusted to know that Grace is yours," she says. "They obviously know she isn't mine. We could easily say the mother was unsuitable and you took custody. Close enough to the truth, and they wouldn't dig."

I nod. "Okay, so then it's just mine that are the problem."

"Will they notice that she looks like you? She definitely has your ears and eyes."

"They haven't seen me in years."

"All the better to remember how you looked as a

baby." Her eyebrows lift and her head tilts. Damn, that's the expression that gets me every time. I glance at the door, wondering.

"Dell, focus."

And…she knows me too well.

"Okay, for them, let's create a cover story," I tell her. "Say we've dated off and on for two years, had a baby, and that sealed it for us. Don't give specifics. Let them fill in the wrong blanks."

"All right. We can keep some details. Like that we met because I work in your building."

"And that I was a horrible rogue who went out with another woman after we met."

She grimaces. "While I was at home with the baby. Yeah, that will all ring true."

"And that we got engaged recently," I say. "Keep that part of the timeline right."

She nods. "We can even say we bonded over baby shopping."

"Then it's settled," I say, standing up. "Shall we leave Friday, return Monday? Can you miss a day?"

"Sure. It's fine. You think that's long enough?"

"Trust me, it's enough. We can fly out Thursday night, though, if you like."

"Let's do that," she says. "Get Grace acclimated before thrusting her in front of everyone."

"Done," I say.

"Hey," she says. "You *have* told her about Grace, right?"

I pause. I'm busted. "Not yet."

"But she knows about me."

"Yes."

Arianna sighs. "You going to warn her ahead or just bring her?"

"I have no idea. What do you think?"

She leans forward on her desk, and her cleavage is a wonder. I have to look away to stay on task.

"At this point, I say we surprise her," she says. "Say that's what we planned all along. There's no other way to cover for why you've kept her hidden."

She's right. "Surprise it is, then," I say.

I head for the door, then turn back. "I wouldn't pack too fancy. They don't live very well. Trailer, actually."

"You don't help them?"

I shrug. "I tried, early on. They're proud. I did secretly pay for my brother's college." I hesitate. "And there's one other thing."

She looks up, her expression cautious. "Which is?"

"They don't know I changed my name."

I expect her to disapprove, but she bursts out laughing. "Does this mean I get to call you Hasmund all weekend?"

This is the worst. "Apparently so."

She claps her hands like a charmed schoolgirl. "I love it!"

I wave her off. "I'll get the arrangements settled."

She's still laughing as I head back down the hall to pick up Grace.

Chapter 6: Arianna

The moment Dell is gone, I feel deeply chagrined. My parents don't know about my engagement to Dell. I need to fix that.

I have to load up Instagram to track down where my mother resides at the moment. She might not call or send messages about her movements around the globe, but I can count on social media and tagged check-ins to tell me her current location.

Huh. Florida. Some fashion charity event was last night. She went shopping this morning. She's posted pictures of hats she fancies. I figure commenting here will get a response about as fast as anywhere, so I type, "Taking a break anytime today?"

Her response is so immediate I know she's obviously checking her stats a lot. "I make time for you, darling."

That is a public statement, not a real one. I could test her by actually calling, but it's evening there, and she'll probably be having dinner with someone. Instead I text, "Call me when you can. Big news."

She surprises me by immediately ringing my phone. Before I can even say "Hello," she cuts in. "Darling, you are on speaker phone. I have your father here. And the amazing designer Antone York. Plus his lovely partner Da Vinci and some of his senior staff. Is your news sharable to all?"

Wow. That's Mom for you. Her moments need to be public, or they simply don't count.

"Well, it will hit the news soon anyway. I'm getting married. To Dell Brant."

The squeals are so piercing I have to pull the phone away from my ear. They are not my mother's. My mother does not squeal.

A male voice says, "Da Vinci, please, we're in Giacomo."

When my mother speaks, her voice is even and

measured. "It's fine, Antone. He's excited. We all are." Then to me, "That's marvelous, my darling. Have you set a date? And a place?"

"Not yet. It's pretty new."

"We'll have to set aside a few months to plan. Can you take a leave? Are you finally going to sell your little *side business*?"

Whew. I have to breathe deeply to manage my upset. I have to remind myself that this is all Mom knows. Work is dirty. Real work, anyway. Anything more taxing than directing a team of minions is beneath consideration.

"We haven't made any decisions yet. We're meeting Dell's family this weekend and telling them the news."

"Oh? Where are they?"

"Birmingham, Alabama."

I can hear the whispers. Mom says, "Oh, hush now. This is my son-in-law." Then more clearly, "Whatever is in Birmingham that would interest the Brant family?"

"The racetrack, I guess." I need to end this conversation, now, before I blow it.

"Ah, I see. The King family owns a horse track

upstate. I'm sure it's similar. This is so fabulous, Arianna. Now, I've seen some gossip about the baby. Everyone keeps saying it is yours and Dell is adopting. Can you set the record straight?"

Oh, no. She went there. Now she's got an entire audience of people listening in.

"Why don't you come meet her?" I say instead. "We can talk about her then."

"I'll have my assistant call you," she says. "Should we come see Dell's family this weekend too? Make it a party? It's just a hop to Alabama from Florida."

I ask the world for forgiveness for this moment, but for the first time in my life, I show off. "Oh, no, Mother, don't dirty yourself on commercial airlines. We'll get together when Dell can have his pilot fetch us all. Talk soon!"

And I hang up.

Bloody hell.

What a mess this is. Dell and I just discussed fifteen minutes ago what we would tell everyone. But I forgot my mother is the queen of social media. First we have to sell the baby's past in a way that she buys it. I've never had to trust her with a secret, and I can't start now.

I realize how little I know her.

And how serious breaking outside our private little bubble will be for Grace.

For all of us.

Chapter 7: Dell

This flight is literally touching down on a highway to hell.

It's true. Interstate 59 runs alongside the airport. It's a road I got to know well as a teen, as I frequently got asked to drive from the racetrack to the airport to pick someone up.

It was almost never anyone important. Maybe a breeder. Maybe a trainer's family.

The big-money people, the owners and big betters, were handled by someone way classier than me.

I glance over at Arianna, engrossed in her laptop

at the table. And Grace, asleep, strapped in her car seat attached to one of the chairs. It's hard coming back here. I don't want to strut in like I'm big stuff after leaving my humble beginnings behind.

I don't want to be here at all.

But I am.

I should be grateful for the stretch of road I'm about to go down again. Despite my overwhelmingly negative memories of it, there was one exception, one that changed everything.

Roscoe Denny. He was a big-ticket better, coarse and rude. Every image I ever saw of him showed the sixty-year-old sun-weathered ex–ranch hand sucking on a cigar, his beady eyes hidden behind half-dark glasses in the shadow of a straw cowboy hat.

Back then, the racetrack had just phased out live thoroughbred horse racing, leaving only the greyhounds they'd added when I was twelve.

A lot of the wealth and prestige had departed with the horses, and the track was perpetually in danger of closing. We had to court the people with money to bet.

At that time, we had a girl who drove the Mercedes to pick up the bigwigs. Armalina Redding. I had a bit of a crush on her, being only seventeen while she was a worldly twenty-two.

She was beautiful and kind spoken. She could charm anybody and knew the entire history of Birmingham. She'd treat the VIP guests of the track to a little storytelling on their ride over. They got to requesting her by name.

But Roscoe Denny was too much for her. He propositioned her. Made suggestive remarks. He took every opportunity to drape his arm over her shoulders, or place a hand on her waist.

I don't think it ever went any further than that, as at least six of us at the track would have killed him, but she flat out refused to pick him up any longer.

And so one fateful day my senior year of high school, the track manager called me over and asked me to pick up Roscoe Denny.

I was still smarting over Frank Leon getting the newest lead-out position when it should have been mine. Frank hadn't done squat at the track other than take up space. But his dad was a trainer, unlike mine, who cleaned up after dogs. He got the opening.

So I might have had a chip on my shoulder that day I drove the car over to the airport, between Frank getting my job and this Roscoe asshole putting the moves on Armalina the last time he was in town.

I sat in the pickup lane, punching buttons, trying to figure out the fancy features of that 1998 Mercedes. You didn't have to put a key in the door to unlock it. The sunroof opened with a mechanical whir. And it didn't just have a CD player, but one that could hold six CDs at one time and change them out.

I fiddled with this, moving between the Backstreet Boys, Celine Dion, and LeAnn Rimes, my annoyance rising. Who picked these? I settled on the radio.

My instinct was to tell this Roscoe guy where he could stuff himself, upsetting a sweet girl like Armalina. She was perfection, and he was bullshit. I was tempted to shovel a round of dog shit onto the backseat to smear his fancy-ass suit and improve his stink.

My mood didn't improve when some airport stooge banged on my window and told me I was supposed to be outside to open the door for my charge. I had to futz around to even figure out how to unlock the dang thing.

But Roscoe laughed the guy off and jumped in.

"No bags," he said to me. "We can hightail it on out of here."

Which I did, the minute the door closed again.

"What a heel," Roscoe said. "Thinks he's important when he's nothing but the dirt people tread on as they go real places."

I didn't expect this. I had half wondered if he was going to be pissed that I wasn't Armalina.

"What's your name, boy?" he asked.

I hesitated, as I always did. Hasmund didn't shorten to anything. "Mac," I said. I'd tried to get that nickname to stick since grade school, but nobody called me by it.

"Well, Mac," Roscoe said, "you look like you're about to fly the coop. You graduated yet?"

"About to in May," I said.

"I've seen you around the track. You work hard."

"Been with the hounds since I was twelve, and mucked out the horse stalls before that." I circled the airport to head back to the highway. Roscoe wasn't anything like I expected.

"You been a lead-out?"

I grimaced. "Nah. Keep getting passed over." I wasn't thrilled to admit this, but I saw no reason not to lay it out. I figured Roscoe was the sort to know what's up anyway.

"I have never understood why they let those pansy-ass rich boys handle the dogs when it's so critical how they go into the gate. Greyhounds are a whole 'nother kettle of fish than horses."

This was my kind of talk. My hand slammed the steering wheel. "Exactly. Tommy Trueblood totally screwed his dog when he acted so squirrelly loading him that the dog got spooked. He came out of the gate like an unwhelped mutt."

Roscoe laughed, long and loud.

I glanced at him in the rearview mirror. He didn't seem so bad now. I didn't know it then, but I was looking at the face of a good ol' boy. And good ol' boys did right by their kind to the exclusion of everybody else.

Which meant anybody who didn't look and think like him.

These days, I eat good ol' boys for breakfast. I enjoy dismantling the businesses they built on sexism and prejudice and selling them for spare parts.

But back then, all I knew was this man was rich and powerful, and he liked me.

We talked about other random things on that drive. Roscoe laughed a lot more. I didn't know that day was going to change my life until a few weeks later, when I got called in by the racetrack manager. They said Roscoe was giving me a scholarship to Auburn University, as long as I could get accepted.

I spent that year repairing grades and joining clubs, making my application look the way my high school counselor said it should. I got wait-listed at first, but eventually I made it in.

And from then on, I saw how things worked. It wasn't the job you did that mattered, but who you did it for. And I looked for the people who could point me the direction I wanted to go. I'll be the first to admit I was a total bastard, sweet-talking sorority girls who could get me into frat parties where I made friends with people who had CEO fathers.

They all called me Mac.

Roscoe Denny died before I finished my degree. I never saw him again. And I don't admire him as much as feel grateful that he chose me as a project. That first unexpected leg up sent me on my way.

Even if I never did get to be lead-out.

Arianna stretches as we wait for the crew to

prepare to let us off the plane. Grace starts to stir too, no longer lulled by the gentle motion of the flight. It's night here, well past her bedtime. But we still have to settle into the hotel. Tomorrow we meet the parents, and I can't help but dread every moment of it.

Chapter 8: Arianna

The morning dawns bright and clear. The hotel isn't exactly luxurious, but it serves its purpose. Dell and I could have stayed at a resort at the golf course on the outskirts of Birmingham, but I wanted to see the city proper.

So we chose one in the downtown area. Only a handful of buildings stand out on the cityscape. It's rare I stay in a city this small. I like it.

Dell comes up behind me. I try to think of him as Hasmund now so that I don't slip, but the name doesn't come easily after four months. I wonder if he should out himself to his parents, at least. I can't imagine my family not even knowing the name I go by. Mom no doubt subscribes to my Google alerts, even as dull as I am.

Although, maybe not so boring. There's the baby issue, which she will certainly drill me on soon. I swept the issue away on the phone, but I know I'll have to be a little more keen when I see her to settle her curiosity.

"What's got you so serious?" Dell asks, his face nuzzling my neck.

"Just hoping we can keep our story straight," I say.

He grips me more tightly. "There's a lot riding on it."

"What happens if it does get out?" I ask. "We found Grace's mother. And we may have left a trail when we visited Winnie then flew to France."

Dell releases me and perches on the side of an armchair. "No one knows about that affair. But we'll have to be convincing," he says. "We'll limit contact on this trip to direct family. Just a quick meeting, introduce everyone. I plan to draw my mother and brother out by taking them to lunch." He grimaces.

"You don't sound thrilled."

"It's just that they don't have a lot of truly private dining experiences here, and even if they did, I don't think my mother would…" He hesitates. "Fit in."

"What's she like?" I ask. When I think of her, I imagine an aging southern belle, spun gray hair and an apron over her dress. Dell has no pictures of his family in his penthouse.

"Well, I haven't seen her in person in thirteen years," Dell says, "but she's whip thin with wild hair and a million tattoos, and more personality than you should be able to fit into one woman. She's strong, which is why I guess she could deal with my father. I would have walked away years ago. I guess I did."

I turn to look at him. His dark eyes are serious, a crease pinched between them. "What is the deal with your dad? Why do you dislike him so much?"

Dell stares out the window. He's not the same here. Less sure of himself. More vulnerable. In New York, he is a force. Nobody crosses him. He walks with this air of unbreakable tenacity.

But now, I sense his weak spot. He changed his name to shake this town, this history.

He hasn't answered yet, so I step forward and take his hands. They are strong and large and make me feel dainty. The wispy fabric of my silk robe brushes between us.

I love this man. I wonder if half of his womanizing ways were to avoid this sort of family moment. A girl who never gets more than a weekend can't insist on meeting his parents.

"In some ways he was a typical dad," Dell finally says. "Roughhoused with me and Donovan. Taught us baseball. Made us work hard. Forced us to have manners."

He barks out a laugh. "But he was bitter. As we got older, he just expected us to be more than we were. Nothing we did was good enough. Donny was young still when I started working at the racetrack. So he didn't get it as hard. Not that I saw."

He sighs, shaking his head as if he can knock the memories out. "He was a straight-up asshole in the end. Felt I was a loser. A disappointment. Nothing."

My head rests against his chest. "And you never let him know who you became? You didn't want to show him?"

"He doesn't deserve to be a part of it," Dell says, wrapping his arms around my back.

"What do you want your parents to know now?"

I ask. "They might separate us and quiz us individually."

"I have no intention of letting that happen. I plan to invite Mom to a lunch Dad would never show up at, introduce her to the baby, and then go to a park so they can play. Donovan will hopefully bring Mom so he can be with us. And that will be the end of it."

I nod against his chest. "What if she is pushy about us visiting her house or seeing your dad?"

Dell huffs out a laugh. "I've put off dukes and presidents. I'm not going to be bullied by my mother."

"She might not have the worldly influence of a duke or a president," I say, "but she's got the ultimate power over you."

A cry from the adjacent bedroom tells us Grace has awakened.

"I'll get her," Dell says, pulling away.

When he's gone, I sit in the armchair, looking out over the city. This is Dell's stomping grounds. Where he was born. Where he worked so hard. Where he sprang from.

It sounds like his success is more in spite of his upbringing rather than because of it. I wish I could think of a way to help mend the rift with his father.

But I'm not one to talk. I see my own parents once a year at best.

Dell reemerges with a crying, out-of-sorts baby. Poor bub. New place. Off schedule. Hungry and probably wet.

"I'll change her if you can make a bottle," he says.

"On it," I say, heading to the desk with a mini-fridge and a small microwave.

As I mix some formula and dig around the suitcase for the stash of baby food jars, I think over Dell's plan for the weekend. It sounds easy enough.

Lunch.

Park.

Mom. Brother.

No dad.

In. Out. Duty done.

We can do this, easy.

Chapter 9: Dell

I make the call to my mother while Arianna bathes and dresses Grace for her big meeting.

She answers on the second ring. "Hasmund?"

"Yes, it's me, Mom."

"Are you in town already? It's so early!"

"Yes, we're downtown."

"Well, what are you doing there?"

I laugh. "We got a hotel for the night. So, I've got us reservations at La Fontaine downtown at noon." I glance out the window. "It's a nice day, so I thought we could go to one of the downtown parks for a bit."

"Cancel them," Mom says.

"What?"

"Your reservations," she says. "First of all, I don't go nowhere that requires reservations. They're too hoity-toity for me. Second, I already got everybody ready for you. We have a big potluck planned late afternoon when everybody gets off work. Aunt Marge roasted a pig. Been working on it all night. And we got cakes and pies and that corn casserole you used to scarf down."

She almost has me at corn casserole. But then I remember — family. People. Too many.

Grace.

"Mom, we can't do that. We have some really big news for you. It's private."

"Ah, baloney," she says. "Getting married isn't private. We want to tell everybody! We've got the whole thing set up. A regular engagement party. Your cousin Daniel Dean got on his computer and made y'all a fancy sign for congratulations. He's a wizard on machines."

This is a disaster. "Mom, we can't do that. It's too much. Arianna will flip."

"I always knew you were ashamed of your family. Is your bride one of those rich snooty types?"

"No!"

"Well, then shut your bellyaching and be down at the VA Hall at five. And don't give me any more lip about it."

She hangs up.

I stare at my phone. What just happened?

Arianna stands in the doorway with Grace wrapped in a towel.

"Not go according to plan?" she asks. She's careful not to look smug.

I can't even answer. I'm still stupefied that somebody ordered me around. I had completely forgotten what she could be like.

"You okay, Dell?" Arianna steps closer.

"Mom has set up an engagement party for us," I say. "I'm not sure how to get out of it."

Arianna settles on the armchair near me, drying Grace's head. "Maybe you need to rethink the weekend. Reconnect with them." She glances down at Grace. "Let's just hold the ruse, okay? We can do this. We had a relationship, broke up, then found out I was pregnant and decided to try again."

"We'll mess up the details. We don't have the story foolproof." This is a disaster.

Arianna reaches out to touch my arm. "I think it will be fine, Dell. These are people who love you. And it's no big scandal to have a baby before we're married. It happens all the time."

I walk the length of the hotel room. I hate it. It's small. Ordinary. There is nothing to my standards here. This town. This hotel. This life.

Grace coos from the towel. She loves being dried off after a bath.

"Here, give her to me," I say.

Arianna lifts Grace up, and I take her. She smells of baby shampoo and heaven. Her bright eyes look up at me, as innocent and guileless as the moon.

She calms me. Arianna is right. Babies are just babies. The only scandals are the ones done by the adults. And we're doing the right thing here. Getting married. Taking care of her.

I just don't want any of this to reflect badly on Arianna. She's done nothing but save me. And now she's entering a place where she'll be judged.

"This isn't how it's supposed to go down," I say.

"I guess it's time for Hasmund McDonald to realize he doesn't control the world," she says. "There's no Dell Brant here."

Arianna stands and smooths her fitted gray pants. An elegant fluttery shirt in subtle tones looks expensive and classy. She's going to stand out at a Legion Hall potluck.

But she's right. I have no control here. If there is anything I've learned from these last conversations with my mother, it's that if I got my domineering, my-way-or-the-highway attitude from anyone, it's *her*.

"Am I overdressed?" she asks.

"Is that an Armani blouse?" I ask.

She looks down at it. "Yes."

"And pants?"

"Isabel Marant Étoile," she says. "A gift from my mother."

"I guess you know that outfit is two house payments down here."

She plucks at her shirt. "Do I have time to shop somewhere more appropriate?"

"No, I love you just as you are. Just know that everyone you meet will buy their things at Wal-Mart."

"I've never been in a Wal-Mart," she says. "Do they have them in Manhattan?"

"Manhattan, Kansas," I say wryly.

"Maybe I should go," she says. "I could stand to

learn a little culture. Broaden my horizons."

This makes me laugh out loud. "Sure, okay. Let's make sure we squeeze that in."

She frowns. "Are you making fun of me?"

I switch Grace to one arm and wrap the other around Arianna. "Not in a million years. I'm making fun of me. And I'm not any more fit to walk into this party than you are."

"We'll be gracious," she says. "You and I are the epitome of manners."

"That's a good thing," I tell her. "Because we're about to be tested."

She takes Grace from my arms and heads back to the adjoining room, where we've stored all of the baby's things. I glance around the cramped room. I should be fitting back into the land where I grew up.

But instead I find it stifling, unfamiliar, and if I'm willing to admit it, scary as hell.

I have no idea how they will treat Arianna. Maybe I should have her dress more plainly. But it is an engagement party. People will pull out their best.

At this point our best hope is that Grace steals the show.

And that my father doesn't show up.

Chapter 10: Arianna

We eat at the lovely restaurant Dell had chosen for his family. It's precisely our style and I feel perfectly at home.

Afterward, though, we go to Railroad Park. It's a pretty scenic area of downtown with walking paths. There, I start to see what he means. I'm overdressed. Most of the mothers have on jeans or some form of workout clothes. I wonder what this VA Hall is like. The restaurant or the park? Which way do I dress?

Back at the hotel, I quickly look up the VA Hall and the American Legion. These look like very honorable organizations devoted to veterans and national pride. It might be a little dated, sure, but I can see that everyone in the pictures looks friendly.

But they're all in jeans and normal shirts. The old men wear their ball caps with words on the front describing their service.

Okay, so my couture outfit is all wrong.

Dell didn't even bring any of his own trademark suits. Just jeans and button-downs.

So I change into something plainer, navy stretch pants and a long loose sweater. This is better. I'm determined to fit in.

This will be fine.

Still, by the time five approaches and Dell requests our car to be brought around, my stomach is filled with butterflies. It's bound to be hard to meet your future in-laws. But we have a surprise baby and a secret to shield.

I plan to stay glued to Dell's side.

Hasmund. Hasmund. I have to think and say *Hasmund.*

"What if I gave you some nickname?" I ask as we wait for the car.

Dell shifts Grace in his arms. She's fussy, as if our anxiety is fueling hers. "Like what?"

"I don't know. Honey Bear or Sweetie Pie or something."

This makes a small smile appear. "Honey Bear?"

"I'm just sure I'm going to call you Dell accidentally."

"Maybe the nickname should be Dellish, then," he says. "I could be called Dell-icious."

"Oh, Dell. Hasmund. Honey Bear." I trip over all the words.

He wraps his free arm around me. "It's going to be fine."

"No, I'm going to screw this up."

"You can call me Doodles," he says.

I sputter my reply. "Like what Grace does in her pants?"

"Okay, maybe not."

An SUV pulls up, white and nondescript.

"This us?" I ask.

"Yes, just what I asked for."

There isn't a porter to open the door, so Dell does it himself. The valet runs around. "Here you go!"

Dell hands me Grace. "I'll get the car seat locked in."

I sit on the front passenger side, Grace on my

lap. "You ready for an adventure?" I ask her.

She drools down her chin in response. Teething.

She wears classic pink, a little checked dress with a matching sweater. Is it too much? Can a baby be overdressed?

I'm unsure about everything now.

"All ready," he says.

He looks like a normal dad, his hair falling from its perfect wave over the exertion of installing the seat. We're a long way from having a driver, a butler, and people who do those sorts of things for us.

It's good. It feels real. I pass him Grace and he buckles her in. The seats are fabric instead of leather. The dashboard is simple. A base model car. It seems right. We shouldn't be ostentatious.

Dell gets behind the wheel.

"You remember your way around?" I ask.

"This town isn't that big," he says. "But I have noticed some changes. A few more tall buildings. The park was different."

"This Legion Hall, do you know it?"

"Like the back of my hand. My uncle Travis was in Vietnam, so the whole family practically lives up there. They do a lot of suppers and events. It's like the social hub of my neighborhood."

I settle back in the seat. This will be fine. Like a reception. Food, drinks, people chatting at tables. Nothing I can't handle.

We drive away from the hotels and office buildings of downtown and out among normal neighborhoods and businesses. I'm eager to see the city where Dell — Hasmund — grew up.

Doodles. I snort a laugh.

"I'm glad you're feeling relaxed," Dell says. "We can work this room. We'll have them all well in hand."

"Recap," I say. "We've had an on-and-off-again relationship but are committing now."

"Other facts stay the same. You own a daycare," he says. "And I work in finance."

"What about pictures? What if people upload things and comment? Nobody knows Grace is yours."

"Hasmund McDonald doesn't exist. They can type that name in all they want."

"But Arianna Hart does."

"We'll avoid giving anyone your last name."

"But what if someone who knows you as Dell sees a picture?"

"Seems unlikely."

"But if anybody does…" I glance at the backseat.

He frowns. "All right. I think I'm missing an accessory." He peers out the window. "If it's still there, I should see…" He turns the wheel. "Yes."

We exit the highway and pull into the parking lot of a gas station. The place is enormous and the lot is filled with eighteen-wheelers. I glance up at the sign. Flying J Truck Stop.

"I'm just going to run in right quick," he says.

I've never seen a place like this before. I turn around to look at Grace, but she faces backward and we don't have a mirror installed. I can see her kicking, though, fingers reaching for the toys hanging from the canopy.

After a moment, Dell emerges from the store holding a ball cap. He tugs the tag off and tosses it in a trash bin as he approaches the car.

When he gets in, I ask, "A hat?"

"Totally in line with the company," he says, dropping the car into reverse to get us out of the lot. "And will totally keep me incognito in any pictures."

"Isn't it rude to wear hats indoors?" I ask.

"Only during prayers and the National Anthem," he says. "Otherwise, fair game at all times."

Wow, okay. "I feel like I need a handbook."

He laughs as we start navigating back roads. "Oh, trust me, there are no rules other than that there are no rules."

This does not make me feel better. I pluck at the sweater, feeling warm despite the season. Maybe I should run into the truck stop and buy an outfit.

Dell picks up my hand from my lap and lifts it to his lips. "Don't fret, Arianna. Remember that at the end of the day, we walk away."

I try to feel more confident with his assurances. But my brain wants to argue. There's holidays ahead! And a wedding!

I start to think we should elope.

Chapter 11: Dell

When Arianna and I pull up to the American Legion Hall a little after five, it's clear there is a party in full swing.

Cars are parked all over the lot and in the dirt beside it and along the street.

I stand by the open door of the SUV, feeling a little more concerned than I did earlier. Is half of Birmingham invited to this shindig?

Did the word shindig *just jump into my head?*

I shake it off and close the door, coming around to the other side for Grace.

Arianna steps out, smoothing her sweater. She

looks anxious.

I reach in for the baby and unbuckle her. She's kicking and waving her arms. A good mood. That's one less thing to worry about.

The diaper bag gets caught between the seats, and I have to tug to get it out.

"Everything okay?" Arianna asks, coming around the door.

"All good." I take a second to arrange the baby in my arms and the bag on my shoulder.

Our diverted attention means that when we turn around, we're blindsided by two pairs of legs and hands, and two shirts thrust near our faces.

One says "Groom" in ironed letters. The other reads "Bride."

"And look on the back," says a voice I can't quite place. There's a flash of a grin before the shirt flips. The back says "I'm with the ball." And the other reads "I'm with the chain." With arrows pointing at each other.

Now the shirt comes down. It's Aunt Marge. Her lips are a florid orange, just a shade off her fluffy spun hair. "Love 'em or what?"

The other shirt comes down. It's Daniel Dean,

my cousin, Marge's son. He's a redneck through and through, his cheek bulging with chewing tobacco, his face rough with stubble, and his gimme cap curved tight over his forehead.

"She's got a way with an iron," Daniel Dean says, looking at the shirt. "The backs were my idea."

I bet they were. I glance over at Arianna.

She has the biggest, fakest, most wide-eyed expression I've ever seen on her.

"How…lovely," she says. "So much work went into them."

Marge turns her "bride" shirt around. "I messed up the 'b' a bit, but *bride* or *ride*, it's all about the same, isn't it?" She elbows Arianna.

"Yes," Arianna murmurs.

"This is my aunt Marge," I tell Arianna. "And her son, my cousin Daniel Dean."

"Nice to meet you," Arianna says.

"Great gift, thanks," I tell them, taking the shirts and tossing them over my arm.

"Oh, you have to wear them," Daniel Dean says. "Everybody's expecting it! They've all got their cameras ready to go!"

"Oh, I couldn't risk messing it up!" Arianna says.

"I might spill something on it."

"Nonsense," Aunt Marge says. She snatches the "bride" shirt from me and drags it over Arianna's head.

I hear a little yelp. Arianna's face pops through the hole. Her hair is all over the place, curls springing out from the careful updo she'd put together. Marge tugs the shirt down. It's tight over the bulk of her sweater and makes Arianna look like a sausage.

She puts her game face on, though. "Thank you," she tells Aunt Marge.

Daniel Dean steps up to force one on me, then seems to realize I'm holding a baby. "Who is this little critter?"

"This is Grace," I say evenly. I don't have to give anything away.

But Marge gets excited. "Yours, hers, or both?" she asks.

My gaze meets Arianna's. "Both," I say.

"By gawd, you better get yourself hitched!" she shouts, so loud it makes me blink. "Gotta make an honest critter out of this one!" She turns around to the open front door of the hall. "Wynona, get your tail out here! You're a grandma!"

Mom sticks her head out the door. It's the first time I've seen her in over a decade, but she doesn't look much different from a distance.

"What are you going on about? You're ruining the big entrance!"

"Git on out here!" Marge calls. "You gotta see this!"

Mom emerges. As she comes down the front walk, I can see she's changed, her face more weathered and lined. Her hair is wiry with gray mixed in the brown. She's dressed up for her, trading her cut-up T-shirts and tank tops for a blue long-sleeved shirt and jeans. Someone's pinned a flower on her shoulder. Barefoot, though, as usual.

"Come look at this kid," Daniel Dean shouts back at her. "Didn't you know Hasmund had a kid?"

Mom stomps down the steps, her feet slapping against the wood. "Hasmund does not have any kid. He would have—" She stops short when she sees Grace. "Who is this?"

"It's Grace, Mom. We wanted to surprise you. She's eight months old." I pick up Grace's hand and give it a little wave.

This part surprises me. Mom's eyes tear up, and

she bites her lip. Her voice loses its caustic quality. "Well, look at her," she says, holding out her arms. "Can I see her?"

I glance over at Arianna, who nods fervently. I pass the baby over, wondering if she'll get fussy with a stranger.

But Grace has that sober look she gets when she's taking in something new. She gazes up at Mom with a curious, intense expression.

"Well, if this don't beat all," Mom says, her voice cracking.

She smooshes Grace's cheek against her own. "Beautiful little stinker. Eight months old." She tilts her head. "So back in April?"

"April 6," I say.

Mom holds her up. She can't stop staring. "Just look at her. Marge, you ever seen anything so pretty?"

"Don't think so," Marge says. "You and I had nothing but grubby ol' boys."

From the entrance to the hall comes "What's going on out here?"

I would know THAT voice anywhere. We turn to see Grandma Jessie, the mother of Marge and my mom, coming down the ramp in her wheelchair.

Uncle Travis, Marge's husband, pushes her.

She holds a cane despite the chair and waves it around. "What's this I hear about a baby?"

"You got your first great-grandchild right here, Mama," Mom says, holding up Grace. "Hasmund didn't tell nobody."

"Look at that baby girl," Grandma Jessie says. "Give her to me." She passes the cane to Uncle Travis.

Mom sets Grace in her lap. Grace has had just about enough of this and no more gets settled when she lets out a lusty howl.

"Hear them lungs!" Grandma Jessie says. "She's a Spencer, all right!"

I come forward to take her, but Grandma waves me off. "I done raised two girls of my own. I can handle this." She jiggles Grace on her knee. "What's wrong with your daddy, not telling nobody you were born?"

She peers up at me. "I'm going to take my cane to you when I set down this child. You better run."

I don't even know how to address half the comments that have been made in the past two minutes. The jiggles work on Grace, and soon she's giggling and babbling and reaching for Grandma Jessie's big God's-eye necklace.

"Well, don't just stand around gawking," Daniel Dean says. "I'm starving and Mom wouldn't let me touch that pig until you saw it."

"It's turned all brown and perfect," Marge says. "Purtiest pig I ever roasted, if I may say so myself."

"And you may," Mom says, clapping Marge on the back. She finally seems to notice the two of us. "Well, Hasmund, go ahead and introduce me to your bride."

Arianna puts on a pleasant expression, her curls all over the place, the T-shirt stretched over her clothes. She's a trouper.

"Mom, this is Arianna. She owns a daycare in New York."

"Call me Wynona," Mom says. "My friend Rhonda down the street owns a little daycare herself. Operates it out of her house. I 'spect you two will have a lot to talk about."

"I'm sure we will," Arianna says. She shakes Mom's hand. "I enjoy being around children."

"Got plenty of those around here!" Marge says, shoving Daniel Dean. "And sometimes they turn twenty-four and still don't leave home!"

"Aw, Ma," Daniel Dean says.

I take Arianna's hand in mine. Uncle Travis starts pushing Grandma Jessie, still holding on to Grace, back up the walk. We fall in step behind them.

Arianna plucks at her shirt. I know she doesn't want to go in wearing it, but she's stuck. The least I can do is show solidarity. I let go of her and pull my shirt over my head.

When in Alabama, you do what your mama tells you.

Chapter 12: Arianna

I'm pretty used to feeling inadequate in situations. There was high school, where nobody would date frizzy-headed, low-self-esteem me.

Then college, where I got some begrudging respect for my family name, but the boyfriends were more about social climbing than wanting me for me, and I never felt comfortable around anybody. I was always…less.

But even with all that, I've never walked into a party wearing a ball-and-chain T-shirt where every single person in the room thinks I got knocked up and tied down the father on purpose.

I'm trying to feel fine.

Dell and I walk in to a headache-inducing blast of cell phone camera flashes. I hope his hat helps hide him.

Despite our determination to stay together, we're instantly separated by a sea of huggers.

I'm drowning in perfume and the smell of fried food and beer. Arms come around me from every direction. It's an endless parade of them.

They say random things like "Glad to meet ya" and "Can't believe Hasmund's come home finally!" Their voices become a long ramble of words. I hug and nod and hug and nod.

At one point, I spot Dell's head across the room, but I can't get to him. There's fifty people between us, easy, plus something else.

The pig.

It's on display in the center of the room, still stuck in both ends by the rod on the spit. I have to turn away from its face.

Now, I love ham. And pork chops. And my hips are no doubt rounded out by a fair share of bacon. But seeing the pig itself is another thing altogether.

I might have just become a vegetarian.

With the initial rush of greetings past, the bulk of the crowd drifts toward the beer keg.

I think I'm free and can find Dell, but then I'm surrounded again, this time by a half-dozen women. And questions start launching like rockets.

"What do you do, dear?"

"What sort of name is Arianna?"

"Have you set a date?"

"Will you get married here in Birmingham?"

"How did you two meet?"

I answer as best I can, following our script and scanning the room for Grace. There's plenty of little kids running amok. Just no wheelchair, and no baby. I feel a brush of panic starting to sweep across my belly. I've been separated from her too long.

Daniel Dean jumps up on a counter and bangs on a cowbell. "Attention! Listen up!"

When everyone turns to him, I slip through the crowd toward Dell.

"Seen Grace?" I whisper when I get to him.

He points toward the back of the room. "She's the star of the show."

I look that way. The Legion Hall is dark paneled and expansive, two big rooms partially divided by a kitchen with large open walls for serving. Antlers and framed flags and proclamations cover the walls. The light is yellow and a bit sickly.

Grace is still on Dell's grandmother's lap, but they've been rolled onto a small stage with flags on either end. A steady line of admirers approach to see the baby, completely ignoring Daniel Dean's rousing speech.

Which I should probably be paying attention to.

Now that I know Grace's whereabouts, I turn back to Dell's cousin.

"And furthermore, since my cousin already done gone and knocked the girl up, and the kid turned out better lookin' than his ugly mug…" He pauses for laughter. "We just want to say, congratulations Hasmund and Arianna. Hasmund, my cousin, welcome to life with just one woman for the rest of your livelong days!"

God. I plaster a smile on my face. Daniel Dean approaches the pig. "Let's eat!" he proclaims.

Dell's mother approaches. "I do not know why that cousin of yours thinks he is in charge," she says to Dell. "Are you going to speak to your father?"

I can feel every muscle in Dell's body tense up.

"Not if I can help it," he says.

Wynona grabs his arm, as if to drag him over, when a friendly looking man and his wife approach. They are mid-sixties, dressed well, him in a pair of khakis and a golfing shirt. His wife has well-styled hair and a flowing floral tunic over slim pants.

"Hasmund, I've been wondering what happened to you." The man takes Dell's hand and shakes it vigorously. "I tried to look you up after you graduated Auburn to see if you were back in town, but I couldn't find you anywhere."

"I'm not much for social media," Dell says smoothly. He's still tense, but less so than with his father. I recognize the stance. The one he uses for business dealings, places where he feels comfortable and in control.

"I'm Theresa," the woman says, taking my hand. "Beck is the chief manager for the racetrack. We've known Hasmund since he was small."

Once they approach us, we become surrounded by other people from the track. They're all kind spoken and calm, from the management to the cooks and cleaners. I begin to realize with great relief that most of the Alabama people are perfectly normal, kind and well spoken.

Just not the ones from Dell's family. It's easy now to see the gap between where he came from and who he wanted to become.

I'm figuring him out.

After a few minutes, I excuse myself and make my way to the stage. Grace is overdue for a bottle, and her evening witching hour is approaching.

But she's not there. Grandma Jessie finally gave the baby over to Wynona, who shows her off to another group of women off to one side. Grandma Jessie apparently likes her place of honor on the stage, and has Daniel Dean and his father fetching her beer and slabs of pork. A ring of bottles surrounds her like a fairy circle.

I'm about to reach Wynona's group when a hand grabs my arm. I turn and stare into the face of a man who could only be Dell's father. They have the same chin, same eyes, same heavy brow. This man's hair is still thick and full, but peppered with gray.

Is this how Dell will look in twenty years?

The rugged handsomeness holds up well, but there is a tightness around this man's mouth that Dell doesn't have. And the way of dressing. He's wearing jeans and a checked flannel shirt thrown over a T-shirt bearing the silhouette of a naked woman on a motorcycle.

"Hasmund always did like his women a little stout," he says.

A heat rises in my neck and face. I press against the T-shirt self-consciously. I had imagined a lot of ways my first conversation with Dell's father could go. But this wasn't it.

I already agree with Dell — this man is an ass.

He doesn't know I've figured out who he is. I can move on. I turn to do just that, when I'm stopped again by a hand to my arm.

"Sorry, I should introduce myself." He steps in front of me. "I'm Byron, Hasmund's dad. He's a real chip off the ol' block."

"Hello," I say, trying to keep my chin up and my voice steady. "I'm Arianna."

"So you're getting hitched to my boy," he says. "You know what you're getting into?"

I'm not sure what he's trying to say. "We've known each other quite a while, Mr. McDonald," I say, purposefully not calling him Byron. "I'm quite sure I know."

"He doesn't come around much," Byron says. "What's he do? Where's he livin'?"

I steal a glance across the room. Dell is still caught in the middle of the racetrack crew. They are drawn to his charisma and confidence. He hasn't noticed me with his father.

"We live in New York," I say. "Near Central Park. Dell works in the financial industry."

"Who did you say?" he asks.

Oh my God. I've already done it. Said his name. I'm rattled.

"He does business with Dell," I say quickly. "They sell computers."

"Ah, all right." Byron scratches the side of his head. "So he sells computers?"

"Something like that," I say.

"You do anything, or do you suck the teat of the government?"

Oh, gosh. Well. Wow.

"I run a daycare," I say.

"Huh. We got a neighbor that does that."

Grace lets out a little wail, and my urgency to get away hits a peak.

"It was nice to meet you," I say. "I should get the

baby from your wife."

"Baby?" he asks, but I'm already walking away. I'm surprised nobody's filled him in.

"Just in time," Wynona says, passing me Grace. "She's got a full diaper and I already done my time with Pampers."

I take Grace, feeling my anxiety drop the moment she's in my arms. "I'll get her changed," I say. I glance back to see if Dell's father has followed us.

But he's back with a group of cronies, other men with their beer bottles and loud laughter.

"I see you met Byron," Wynona says. "How did that go?"

I'm not sure if I should be honest or not. "Fine. He wanted to know where we lived."

"I told him you two were in New York. That man doesn't listen."

I nod and take a step back, anxious to get back to Dell. He still has the diaper bag.

"I'll just get her changed," I say again, hoping it gets me away this time.

Wynona folds back into the gaggle of women.

I push through people, glad Dell is tall enough I

can spot him pretty easily.

I'm stopped again by Daniel Dean, who steps in front of me.

Don't these people ever do anything politely?

"I need to change her," I say.

"But it's time to initiate the new McDonald-to-be."

My stomach trembles a bit. "I really want to get to Hasmund," I say carefully. I won't drop the wrong name again. I can see why Dell doesn't want any of them to know it.

"I can see you two are tight," Daniel Dean says. His mother has arrived.

"Ma, you change the baby," he says. "It's initiation time."

She tries to pluck Grace from me, but I turn to the side.

"No," I say firmly. "I will change her and then you do whatever ritual you have planned. She needs a diaper and a bottle first."

Daniel Dean lifts both hands in the air like he's being arrested. "Whooee, Hasmund's got himself a live one!" he says.

"You leave that girl alone," Marge says. "She's

got enough on her hands being around the entire Birmingham clan."

"Hasmund isn't talking to any of us," Daniel Dean says. "He's talking to the track people. And not the shit-shovelers, either. Management. Like he's too good for us."

"Let him be," Marge says. "Let's go get some of Trixie's banana pudding."

That gets him. His eyes light up and he rubs his belly. "I have to get it before Xander eats it all. We'll catch up with you later," he says with a wink.

I doubt that. When I get to Hasmund — Dell — I'll be asking exactly how long we have to be here before we can graciously escape.

Because I am ready to leave *right now*.

Chapter 13: Dell

I'm done here.

Arianna looks frantic and flustered, her face red beneath a tousled halo of curls. I get the sense that someone's really gotten to her, and it's not hard to figure out who, between my crude cousin, my call-it-like-it-is mother, and no telling who else.

"Grace needs a change," she says, holding out her hand for the diaper bag, which is still over my shoulder.

Instead of passing it off, I excuse myself from the racetrack crowd and walk with her to the bathrooms.

"You didn't have to come with me," she says, her

voice flat. "I just needed an escape." She gestures toward the "Women" sign. "I'm quite sure the men's restroom doesn't have a changing table."

"Let's go in here," I say, and steer her toward the office door instead. There's a meeting room off the back, and we can get away from the madness for a while.

Maybe escape out the window.

I'm hoping we've made a clean getaway from the crowd, but as I close the door, I see Daniel Dean has spotted us and lifted his spoon in a salute. Great.

We pass a desk and a door to another, smaller office. Then the meeting room. I open the door to that, and we pass through. I close and lock it.

"Good," Arianna says. "Keep your cousin out. He wants to do some initiation."

My brow crumples. "I don't remember any initiation."

"Well, he's sure there is one."

She takes the diaper bag from me and tugs the padded blanket from the side. Grace seems calmer away from the party. Arianna straightens her out on the pad and pulls off the pink diaper cover that matches her dress.

"How's Grace?" I ask, leaning over her.

She reaches up with her little hands, her feet in tiny white socks coming up to my neck.

I shift aside so Arianna has more room to change her.

"I might be sorry I asked to meet your family," Arianna says.

"I might be sorry I let them anywhere near you," I reply.

We look down at Grace. Arianna whisks away one diaper and bundles her into a fresh one.

"She's bound to be hungry," Arianna says.

"We can hide back here and feed her." I pick Grace up and hoist her to my shoulder.

Arianna empties a formula packet into a bottle and shakes it. "And then?"

"We skedaddle."

This makes her laugh. "Skedaddle. I thought they only used that word in movies."

"It's a perfectly good word," I say, relieved to see the tension leaving her face. "Like, let's skedaddle to the opera for *La Traviata*."

More laughter. I feel my own shoulders relaxing.

Arianna puts on a snooty expression. "Or,

'Darling, shall we skedaddle to the Guggenheim for the children's charity dinner?'"

"See? It's the perfect word."

I set Grace on her feet on the conference table. She bounces, holding my hand, loving the feeling of standing, if only for a moment. When she sees the bottle, she lets go to reach for it.

"Whoa, baby girl," I say as she almost tumbles. "You're not quite ready to be upright."

"She's getting there," Arianna says. "She'll be walking before we know it."

Grace settles onto my arm, holding the bottle with both hands. When did she stop letting us feed her? The transition had been sudden. The sense that her baby time is escaping becomes so strong that I take the bottle from her little hands.

She lets me, content to fall back against the crook of my elbow and let me do the work. I let out a sigh of relief as she continues to drain the bottle. Dang, she can do it fast now.

"Where does the time go?" I ask Arianna. She's putting away the supplies.

"It's quick," she says, tucking the pack of wipes into the bag. Then she plops down onto a cracked vinyl chair next to me.

"Dreary place, isn't it?" I ask. The room is the same dull yellow as the main hall with dark paneled walls. At the end is a whiteboard, the ghostly colors of long-ago messages staining the surface.

"Oh, I don't know. I think it serves its purpose," Arianna says. "Not everything has to be shiny." She brushes a cluster of crumbs from the tabletop and grimaces.

"I've been here a lot," I say. "I hid in this office to escape my family more than once."

"Some things never change," she says, plucking at the "bride" shirt.

"Sorry they accosted you before you could even get your bearings," I say. "I should have predicted that."

"We need a bodyguard," she says with a laugh. "To protect us from your cousin."

"He's not going to pull anything on me," I say. "I'd like to see him try."

"I think he remembers a version of you that is quite different from how you are now."

Grace finishes the bottle, and I pull it away before she sucks air. I lift her to my shoulder. "Well, he has another thing coming if he thinks he's going to initiate you into anything." I pat Grace's back. "I did that myself, I do believe."

Arianna smiles. "I do believe you did."

Grace lets out her trademark sailor belch and laughs, her legs kicking against my chest. I slide her down. "That's all you got?" I ask.

She laughs and pummels her little fists against my chin. I recoil as if it's a punch. "You pack a mean hit, little tiger."

"So now what?" Arianna asks, reaching for the baby. "Do we brave the masses?"

"I think we're done here," I say, standing and shouldering the bag. "We met the fam, showed off the kid. Let's call it a day."

"I didn't see you talk to your father," she says.

This makes my jaw tense. "I have no intention to." We head for the door.

"But you came all this way."

"To see my mother," he says. "And because you asked to meet her."

"Them," she says. "And I talked to your father."

My hand stills on the doorknob. "What did he say?"

Her hesitation says everything.

I turn to her. "Did he insult you? Did he say something about Grace?"

"He didn't see Grace that I know of. I was on my way to fetch her from your mom."

"What did he say to you?" My anger is rising to the red zone.

"Just asked if I sucked the teat of the government," she says, but I can tell there is more by the way she focuses on Grace, holding her hand and making a silly face to avoid saying anything else.

"We are done here," I say, opening the door to the conference room.

"But it's our party," she says.

"No, it's their party, and we're their excuse."

We head back through the office. But when we open the outside door, a mob is there waiting.

Daniel Dean stands close, arms crossed, hands placed so it looks like he has biceps. Aunt Marge and Mom flank him on either side.

Grandma Jessie's there with her wheelchair and cane. And the whole Spencer clan, plus a few on the McDonald side. Other than my dad. Thankfully, he's skipped this part of the festivities.

"Took ya long enough," Grandma Jessie says. "Although, I guess if he takes his time, that's good on you." She winks at Arianna.

"We were changing the—" Arianna attempts, but her words are cut off by the blast of an air horn. Everyone covers their ears. Grace howls and starts to cry.

One of the kids, no telling whose, takes off holding the horn. A woman runs after him, shouting, "Rodney Jay Johnson, get back here right now!"

Mom shakes her head. "She's got to get a handle on that boy."

"It's time for us to go," I say, putting my hand on Grace. Arianna jiggles her to try and settle her after the scare.

"What?" Mom says. "We haven't even started dancing yet. And I didn't see you eat a bite of that pig Marge slaved over."

"We're vegetarians," I lie. "No thanks."

"Oh, no," Daniel Dean says. "Initiating begins now, and we got the music all ready."

I'm done with this lunkhead cousin. I stand close to him in my most intimidating stance. "Step aside."

But he just laughs. "I don't know where that

works, but this here's family, cuz. We don't respond to threats."

Arianna gasps and I turn to see that Aunt Marge has taken the baby again. Daniel Dean grabs Arianna's hand and pulls her toward the dance floor.

I see red. I'm about to pound this asshole into the ground when Mom takes my arm. "Just roll with it, Hasmund. It's all in good fun."

"Neither of us find this fun, Mother."

"You gotta lighten up," she says. "The big city is making you all uptight." She stands beside me, holding on with both hands.

Some teen I don't know sits at a table with a receiver wired to two tall speakers on either side of the stage. After a second, the sound blasts out. A polka.

A bunch of the boys and men are on the floor in a circle. Daniel Dean delivers Arianna to the middle of them and lets her go.

She looks around at them. To her credit, she stands tall and self-assured. I'd be busting some balls.

The men stamp one foot with alternating claps. Then they launch into a side step, making the circle go around her. A few head the wrong way initially, and are shoved into the right direction.

This keeps up for a little bit, and Arianna gamely claps to the music, her white "bride" shirt ghostly in the bluish stage lights.

The men go in toward her, then back out, and the threat I feel when they converge on her makes it hard for me to stand aside.

My mom grips me like she knows she'd better hold on. The women have started to congregate, filling in the corners.

"You haven't seen this before?" Mom asks. "I'm sure we did it back when you were a kid. When Grandma Jessie's sister Louisa got remarried?"

I shake my head.

"I'm pretty sure you did," Mom says. "You must've forgot."

As they swoosh in and out on her, some vague memory starts to dislodge. I left around the time I would have participated in this dance, judging by who's out there. And I never came back. I would only have seen it done by others.

Daniel Dean swoops in on Arianna, locking his elbow around hers and turning her around. She keeps up at first, but then he pivots and switches, catching her off guard.

But he snags her again, and the next time he switches, she's ready.

"They say you can tell what kinda wife you're gonna get by how she does this dance," Mom says.

I do not give one shit whether she meets their expectations, but I'm mesmerized, watching her pick up the pattern. Uncle Travis moves in to take his turn with Arianna, and Daniel Dean falls back into the circle surrounding her.

The music goes on and on, each man coming in.

"You remember when you're supposed to go out?" Mom asks.

"What?" I have no idea.

"It's coming up," she says. Then she pushes on my back and says, "GO!"

I lunge forward. The circle opens, and I get it. I'm supposed to take the last turn with Arianna.

I haven't paid close enough attention to the turns or the pivots, but it doesn't matter. My flush-faced bride has it on lock, and she turns me and makes sure I stay on the beat.

Around us, the circle dissolves as all the women claim their men. And I remember this part. I never jumped in because I didn't have a girl. You only did the dance if someone would claim you at the end.

Muck-shoveling Hasmund didn't have a girl to dance with at the end, so I never did.

But today, I'm in the center. And I have the best one of them all.

Chapter 14: Arianna

Okay, so the party isn't *all* bad.

After the breathless never-ending song with at least twenty partners, I finally have my Dell. Dancing with him is pure exhilaration.

The young teen handling the music gives us all a breather by playing a slow song. Dell pulls me into his arms.

"You were amazing," he says.

"That was pretty wild. You didn't know they were going to do it?"

"No clue. Mom says I've seen that dance before, but I don't really remember it."

We move together. A fuse pops somewhere, eliciting a gasp, then some sparks. A disco light flickers on overhead, covering the room with bright bits of color. A cheer goes up.

"You think they'll burn the place down?" I ask him.

Dell's voice is a murmur in my ear. "If you don't ignite it first."

Ah, Dell.

We finish out the song, our bodies close together, my head on his shoulder. Light falls over us like confetti. It feels like all the high school dances I missed. Like young love.

When the song ends, everybody claps, and I realize we're the only ones still on the dance floor. Part of the ritual, I guess. I wonder if this is how weddings go around here. For the barest instant, I imagine a reception like this. Homespun. Full of traditions, dancing, and cheers.

Then I shake the thought away. My socialite mother would never allow her daughter to marry at an American Legion Hall.

Funny how our moms rule us, despite our age.

We wander through the crowd, everyone

subdued with a meal and a dance under their belts. Dell spots Grace back on Grandma Jessie's lap, so we move to the food table. We've settled in now, our discomfort at bay.

Aunt Marge hands us plates of pork and casserole and sliced fruit. We sit on metal folding chairs, eating from our laps, ignoring that Dell said we were vegetarians. It smells too good, and we're too hungry. We're no longer the focus of attention, my "initiation" over, I suppose.

I take a bite of the smoked meat and almost swoon. The pork I've always known involved tiny circles of loin surrounded by springs of parsley. At least until I discovered bacon, a secret withheld by my model-slim mother.

"How did you not weigh a thousand pounds with this sort of cooking around?" I ask Dell.

"They only break out the pig on a spit for special occasions," Dell says with a laugh. "Otherwise my family lives pretty close to the bone, as they say."

"If this is the bone, I'll cozy up to it." I take another bite.

"It is sort of nice to have someone else watching the baby," he says.

"Maybe it's time to think about a sitter." I take a bite of the strange mushy corn casserole and nearly swoon again. It tastes as rich as sin.

"I guess you have a lot of people you trust we can call on," Dell says. "Maybe it's time to face the outside world."

"What would we do first?" I ask. "The children's hospital charity ball? One of the refugee fund-raisers?"

He laughs. "I can tell you were raised by philanthropists. There's more to life than good works."

I nudge him. "Come on. We have to give back."

"We do, we do. I'm just saying it's okay to simply go out for a cheeseburger."

My fork stabs a slice of cantaloupe. "You were always worried about the photographs."

Dell gestures to the crowd milling around us. "And we just had a thousand taken."

I spin the wedge of fruit on my plate. I'm not sure why I'm resistant to going back out in the world. We've been to parks, and a bit of shopping here and there. But really being out means tabloids and society columns and gossip.

Grace has been a convenient excuse, but when it comes right down to it, I know there is something deeper to my hesitation.

It's hard for me to admit it.

But here it is.

I'm afraid the world will think I'm not good enough for Dell Brant.

Dell sees me staring at my plate and takes it from me. He stacks them on the floor near our feet. "Hey," he says. "What's getting you? My dumb cousin? This whole ridiculous party?"

I shake my head. "No, they're fine. Really. Look how they've taken to Grace."

Daniel Dean has the baby now, dancing her around the floor with the couples making turns to some country song I've never heard.

"For what it's worth, I think they really like you," he says. "But it's hard for me to fit in here anymore." He looks out over the room. "It's like I was never even here."

I take his hand. "Maybe we need to find some sort of middle ground," I say. "We already figured out life didn't have to be work all the time. Maybe it doesn't have to be so formal either. Drive our own cars. Buy our own groceries."

"You're going to use *skedaddle* now, aren't you?" he teases.

"I just might. And I'm rather fond of *git*, aren't you?" I elbow him.

"I'll git you." He grabs my waist and pulls me into his lap.

"You sure this folding chair can hold both of us?" I ask, my mouth near his ear. I almost point out that I'm "stout," but he doesn't know his father said it, and I'm quite sure I'll make things worse if I tell him.

He stands, taking me with him. I'm cradled in his arms.

Daniel Dean sees us and leads a big "Whoop!" followed by cheers. The noise makes Grace pucker up and cry again.

Dell sets me down and walks over to him. "I think it's time for the baby to get some sleep," he says. He takes Grace.

"Ah, Ma can watch the baby. You two stay and dance," Daniel Dean says, waving Wynona over. "We've only floated one of the kegs."

"We have to fly out tomorrow," Dell says.

"Well, that was quick," Wynona says. "I don't reckon you can come over for breakfast tomorrow before you go?"

"Early flight," Dell says. "Got to be at the airport at six."

"Damn," Wynona says. "I guess tickets are cheaper at that hour."

"Gotta save every penny," Dell says.

I have to force myself not to snort with laughter at that.

"Go say good-bye to your father," Wynona says. "You can't come all this way and not even talk to him."

"I can and I will," Dell says. "He and I don't exactly see eye to eye."

"So much bellyaching," Wynona says. "Daniel Dean, go get Byron and tell him to get over here."

I can feel Dell stiffen. "Mom, don't do it. I don't need to talk to him."

"You sure as hell do," she says. "I'm not going to sit here and let you two hate on each other till he keels over." She pulls a pack of cigarettes from her bra, looks around as if realizing where she is, and sticks them back in. "Damn it, you two are the most screwed-up little shits."

Dell turns away from her, shifting Grace to his other arm. "You will not speak that way around my daughter."

"Oh, now I'm not good enough for her." Her voice is sharp, but I can see her eyes have fear in them. She wants to be around Grace. I can only guess that this softer need is at odds with her tough exterior.

Dell doesn't answer that because Daniel Dean comes back with Dell's father.

And when the two men look at each other, I wonder how they are going to avoid coming to blows.

Or if they'll even try to stop themselves.

Chapter 15: Dell

Well, the asshole hasn't changed that much.

In a lot of ways, I'm staring at my own reflection. My father and I are about the same height.

He works hard, so he's fit and broad. His hair is unruly and has gray in it. There's lines around his eyes. He's also darker skinned, as much time as he spends outside.

But basically, I've turned out just like him. On the outside.

"Hello, son," he says. "You don't look a damn thing like your brother."

This takes me off guard. I realize Donovan isn't

at the party. We've been here this whole time and he hasn't shown up.

I turn to Mom. "Where is my brother?"

She shrugs. "I can't keep up with that boy."

"He's got things to do," my father says. "Leave that boy alone."

I see how it is. The favorite son.

My grip on Grace tightens and she protests.

Arianna reaches for her. "Let me have the baby," she says.

I don't want to let her go, but I do. I drop my hands, keeping them loose at my sides. Still, my fists clench.

"You want to hit me, is that it?" my father says. "You never were much of a fighter. Or a worker. Not much of anything."

I hear Arianna gasp.

"Now, Byron," Mom says. "Lay off the boy. It ain't right to play favorites, and I'm done seeing you push my boy away."

"He's the one who done took off and not come back."

"What the hell is wrong with you?" I ask him. "If you think I'm going to let you and your attitude anywhere near my daughter, you can go fuck yourself."

"Language," Mom warns, as if I hadn't corrected her myself just a minute ago. "Show your father some respect."

I'm about to blow, and I know it. "This is not worth it," I say, turning away from him. "Come on, Arianna. Let's go."

"You boys just need to chill," Mom says, darting in front of me. "You can't walk away from this."

"Watch me," I hiss at her.

But Arianna plants her feet, hugging Grace to her chest. "No," she says. "You guys just need to get it out." She glances down at my clenched hands. "Without coming to blows."

"I wouldn't hit my own boy," Dad says. "Even if he has it coming."

I whirl back around. "I don't get it," I say. "I slaved at that damn racetrack every damn day. I did everything everybody told me to, despite bullshit working conditions and nobody respecting anybody there."

"Language," Mom says again, but everyone ignores her.

"Boy, you had an attitude from the moment you could talk," Dad says. "You were too good for this family, always thinking you were above hard work." He gestures at my outfit. "And look at you in your pansy-ass clothes. You think you're better than all of us."

This makes me pause. Had I been that way? Did I look down on the rest of them as soon as I figured out where we stood in the social order?

It was easy to see the hierarchy at a place like the racetrack, where the workers were stratified into hard labor and management.

The McDonalds were at the bottom and never moved.

Why was that?

"I see you working it out in your head," Dad says. "So tell me why I should sit around and have my own kid look down on me."

I have nothing to say to that. My own culpability in this washes over me like a storm. I look at Arianna. She holds Grace close, her eyes full of concern.

"We should go," I tell her. "I think this is broken beyond repair."

"Nonsense," Mom says. She's holding a cigarette

now, obviously dying to light it. "You're just now hashing it out."

But I have nothing else to say. "Come on," I say to Arianna. "Will you come this time?"

She nods. We head toward the door. Most of the party is in the back room, so only a few people have even seen the confrontation. Daniel Dean frowns, his arms crossed, Aunt Marge behind him.

We're out on the front walk when a bright yellow Camaro screeches up to the curb, blaring music. It slams into park, a silence following the cut of the engine.

From behind me, I hear my mother say, "Now he shows."

I catch a whiff of acrid smoke and know she's lit up.

The man who gets out of the car, pausing in the street as he pulls on a sports coat, looks nothing like the dorky kid I last saw.

He's buff, like big-time buff, and walks with a swaggering stride.

"Is that your brother?" Arianna asks. Her eyes are wide. Even baby Grace is staring.

"None other," I say. "He's changed a lot."

"He looks a lot like you," she says. "Different, but alike."

I don't see it, but we stay in the middle of the walk as Donovan comes around the front of his car and finally looks our way.

"Leaving the party already?" he asks, checking his watch. "It's just now time to get things started!"

He heads straight for me. My hand reaches out for a shake on autopilot.

He takes it in his fierce grip and pulls me forward, jerking me into a quick, back-pounding man-hug.

"Damn, you're old, brother!" he says. "And the spitting image of Dad."

He spots Mom behind us. "I thought you said this party would last all night!"

Mom holds her cigarette low. "I didn't count on Hasmund bringing a baby. Look at it. You're an uncle." She blows out a long stream of smoke.

Donovan turns to Arianna and Grace. "Now look at these two beauties." He nods at the shirt. "And a good sport too. That is horrible. I'm sure my cousin foisted it on you." He leans into Grace. "And who are you?"

"My daughter," Dell says. "She's eight months old."

"Gorgeous. And you must be Arianna. Damn saint if you're marrying this sonovabitch." He leans in to kiss her cheek. "It's not too late to run off with me instead."

Arianna laughs, her gaze flicking to me. She's flushed. Finally, a member of my family she actually likes.

Everybody always liked Donovan. Charming and smooth.

He curls his arm around my neck. "There's no way I'm letting you leave your party now. We've got to catch up."

I consider my options as he turns us around. I could protest, leave anyway. But I'm curious about this man who is my brother. And I want to see how my father reacts to him.

Call me stupid, a glutton for punishment, a man who doesn't know when to quit, but damn it all if I don't want to prove my point about my family. To myself, if nobody else.

Mom tosses her cigarette on the ground. "Give me that baby," she says. "Y'all go talk."

"You're going to set the town on fire," Donovan says, crushing the butt with his boot. "We'll give the baby to Aunt Marge until you air out." He kisses her cheek. "Love you, though."

She grabs his head and kisses his cheek back. "I'd quit but I already chose lung cancer as my way to die."

"You're getting there," he says. He turns back to us. "Come on. I heard there was a roast pig, and I aim to eat some."

The party hasn't changed a bit since we left it, other than Dad has melted back into the crowd. "You okay with being here a bit longer?" I ask Arianna.

She hesitates. "Sure. I know you want to spend time with your brother."

When people see Donovan, they immediately smile and smack him on the back. A plate materializes for him. And a beer.

I figured. The favored son.

Aunt Marge takes the baby, promising to rock her in the office and away from the noise. Arianna and I are passed beer too, and slabs of cake.

I want to sit back, take it in, but we're drawn forward with the crowd. Donovan is separated for a second but makes his way back. "Let's find a quiet spot," he says.

We end up in the kitchen area. A cluster of women are scrubbing pans, but there's a table near the back door big enough for three. The din is distant.

"You're getting the hero's welcome," I say. "Same as always."

Donovan waves it aside. "They're happy to see anybody who leaves and comes back. I think they're afraid we'll take all the good out of town and leave them with nothing."

I wonder if that's true.

"You've lost your accent," I tell him.

"You've lost yours too," he says. "Side effect of leaving."

"A good one," I say.

"I rather like the drawl," Arianna says. "It's endearing."

"Our family's got it worse than most," Donovan says, then takes a slug of beer. "It's like they take the normal good people of Birmingham, Alabama, and bring out the worst in themselves."

"I had it out with Dad," I say. "It didn't go well."

"That figures," Donovan says. "One of my first memories is him yelling at you that you weren't shoveling shit the right way. Like there's a nuance to doing it."

This makes me laugh. "I remember."

We stop talking for a bit, Donovan tucking into his plate, washing it down with beer. I can handle this part. It's quiet beyond the crowd and the noise.

Donovan shoves his plate aside. "Mom sure has missed you. 'Bout broke her heart when you never came back."

"Wasn't anything to come back to," I say. "Just bad blood."

Donovan peers at me over his bottle. "I tried finding you a time or two. No trace of Hasmund McDonald anywhere. How did you arrange that?"

Arianna glances at me, her eyebrows raised. I know what she's thinking. That I can tell Donovan. But I don't know that. He seems all right, but I haven't seen him since he was a kid. I have no idea of his allegiances, his level of discretion.

"I tend to work in the background of things," I say. "Financial stuff."

Donovan nods. "I figured you kept things on the down low." He looks over at Arianna. "How did you meet this lowlife?"

She keeps a perfectly straight expression as she says, "We ran in the same circles."

Donovan nods. "And the kid? Both of yours?"

"Yes," Arianna says. "Your brother here took his time deciding to settle down. Grace helped him figure things out."

She's handling things perfectly. Every word she's said is the absolute truth.

"I'm glad to see you settling down," Donovan says, punching me on the shoulder. "Though you never really were a ladies' man."

Arianna chokes on the sip of beer she was drinking, sputtering and coughing. Donovan smacks her on the back. "I know, right! He couldn't get laid in high school if he paid them!"

Arianna wipes her eyes with her fingers. She's having to fight against the laughter. "Lucky for me," she finally gets out.

"Lucky for him, more like it," Donovan says. "Although he ain't half bad now."

I shake my head. "Well, you were a skinny twerp who couldn't even roll the starting box," I say.

He tips his bottle at me. "True that. And I have a picture of myself at age, oh, fifteen, that I leave on my mirror so that every morning when I don't want to get myself to the gym, I'm motivated by my awesome former self."

"Where did you end up going to school?" I ask, even though I know. I sent the checks there.

"Texas. Been thinking of applying to grad school in business, but I might be done with school for the time being."

"You should do it," I say. "There's no skimping on the foundations."

He shrugs. "I need to work a while. Get myself out there."

I figure he can't afford it yet. "There's scholarships."

"I know. I just want to get my hands dirty, you know."

I lean back in my chair. "We did plenty of that at the track."

Donovan tips his bottle again. "True. Very, very true."

A cheer rises up beyond the serving windows, snagging our attention. A line dance has started.

"You should be dancing," Donovan says. "It's your party."

"You know how parties are," I say. "They take on a life of their own."

Donovan stands. "Nah. Let's get out there. I want to be able to make fun of your moves."

I take Arianna's hand and lift her out of her chair. "You up for some Boot Scootin' Boogie?" I ask her.

"I have no idea what that is," she says with a laugh. "But I'm pretty sure I'll go with you anywhere."

We follow Donovan out of the kitchen. I guess when in Rome, you line dance.

Chapter 16: Arianna

The morning after the party, I'm not sure I can move.

I glance at Dell. He's still sound asleep.

My thighs are howling. My feet still hurt. And my head pounds from too many red Solo cups of beer ending up in my hand.

I hear a baby gurgle and look over at the Pack 'n Play to see Grace on her knees, face pressed against the mesh. When she sees she has my attention, she bounces on her knees.

"She's up, isn't she?" Dell asks with a groan.

"Been up a while, by the bright shiny look of

her," I say.

"Huh." Dell presses the heel of his hand into his eyes. "Quite a night, wasn't it?"

"My body thinks so," I say. I squeeze my thighs, trying to calm down the burn. The muscles are tight. "We might have danced more than we're used to."

He laughs. "I don't think we've ever danced."

"There was that one night," I remind him. "In France."

"Oh, yes," he says. "That was an unforgettable night." He turns to me, pressing his mouth against my neck. "That white dress."

His hand roves across my belly.

Grace plops on her bottom and lets out a surprised cry.

His hand stills. "Right. Baby."

We both sit up. And immediately, we both bring our hands to our heads.

"Cheap beer," Dell says. "Let's not do that again."

"You get the aspirin, I'll get the baby," I say.

"Deal."

I rise to a wobbly stance and take uncertain steps toward the Pack 'n Play. I've never been a partyer in any stage of my life, so this feeling is new to me.

I bend down to pick up Grace. She wiggles in my arms, ready to be active and playful. "You hungry, baby girl?" I ask. I hope a bottle will do for now, because I'm not sure I have the patience yet to attempt spooning baby food into her.

Dell returns from the bathroom. "Aspirin and Cheerios," he says, holding up a bottle and a baggie. "I say toss a few in the playpen and go back to bed."

"Aspirin or Cheerios?" I ask. I lift Grace into the air a few times, up and down, getting myself awake and making her giggle.

"I probably couldn't tell the difference."

I take the bag of Cheerios from him and move to the desk. I spread a blanket on it, then drop a few Cheerios. Grace sits wide-legged, leaning forward to grasp the bits in her pudgy fingers. She concentrates hard to get them to her mouth. Every time she makes it, she grins.

I sit in the chair in front of her so she can't escape. The diaper bag is on the floor. I pull a bottle out of the side and mix the formula.

Soon, she's leaning against me, bottle in the air, guzzling like there is no tomorrow. She'll be out of using a bottle soon. We should start transitioning her to a sippy cup.

The idea that her baby time is so fleeting makes my eyes tear up. I sniffle, and Dell comes up behind me.

"You okay?"

"Yeah. It's just what you said last night. It's going fast."

"I think we're doing a good job of putting life on hold for her," he says.

I lay my hand over his on my shoulder. "We are."

Grace drops the bottle and arches her back so she can peer up at us, milk dribbling down her chin. Then she burps spectacularly.

We laugh.

"That's our girl," Dell says, running his hands over her still mostly bald head. "When is she going to get some hair?"

"It'll start coming in soon," I say. "She'll have long pretty locks soon enough, flipping them over her shoulder to look at boys."

Dell groans. "I can't even think about that. God. I'm going to have to strangle them all."

His phone buzzes across the room, so he heads

over. I gather the scattered Cheerios closer to Grace so she can try again to pick them up.

"Hey," Dell says. "I didn't figure you'd be up yet."

I fuss with Grace's sleeper, smoothing down the collar. I wonder who he's talking to. Sounds like someone from the party. His brother? Cousin? Probably not his mother.

"Okay, yes, we're busted," he says into the phone, glancing at the clock. "We're still in town."

I stifle a laugh. Dell had told them we had an early flight. It's after nine.

"Tell her we'll be there. Yeah. Thanks for the heads-up." He ends the call.

"What's going on?" I ask.

"That was Donovan. So they figured out we were lying about the early flight. Dad's off to help set up for tonight's races, but Mom doesn't have to be there until late afternoon. She's made a breakfast thing at the house. Donovan's there, of course. And Marge and Travis."

"So we're going?"

"I guess so. We're here."

I hoist Grace up and turn to him. "I think it's a

good idea to spend a little more time with them. Last night ended up fine."

"I know." He rubs his bristled cheeks. "I want to find out who's hired Donovan anyway. Make sure it's a good company."

The mattress gives as I sit next to him. "I like that you take care of him."

"Our father sure isn't doing it," he says. "I'm going to go shower. I smell like my mother's cigarettes."

He heads toward the bathroom. I lie back on the bed and let Grace crawl around among the sheets. She's happy to be there, navigating the hills of pillows and blankets like she's climbing a mountainside.

Breakfast with the McDonalds. And Spencers. Maybe a quieter, smaller gathering will give me a better feel for how Dell grew up. Just when I think I know him pretty well, I discover a whole new trove of information to study.

Chapter 17: Dell

Driving up to the dilapidated trailer that my family has lived in for forty years isn't easy.

I'm not sure trailers like this are even supposed to last that long. When I was about ten, before Donovan was born, Dad tried to make our home more "permanent" by adding a short wall of cinder blocks around the base to give it the feel of a foundation.

Mom found the whole thing hilarious. She called it putting lipstick on a pig. But when he added a little front deck with a roof where she could sit and smoke outside, she bought into the idea.

I helped build that deck and that roof. When I

last saw it over a decade ago, it was still in decent shape.

So when we pull up, I'm more pleased than I want to admit to see the deck still there. The roof has problems, the corrugated metal warped and coming up in places. Maybe Donovan and I can do something about it after breakfast.

I look over at Arianna to judge her reaction. She's not like me. I grew up here. Humble. Southern. Poor. She has only known Manhattan, Milan, Paris. Fancy lives and money.

"Why are there tires on the roof?" she asks.

Hell of a first question.

"Trailer roofs will rumble in the wind, and eventually leak if you don't."

She nods.

We open our doors and I circle around to unlatch Grace. Even though I got the most basic SUV I could, it still stands out in the trailer park, shiny and new among the rusting battle-axes haphazardly sitting along the gravel lane between the rows.

"Is that a 1995 Cadillac DeVille?" Arianna asks. Her hands are on her cheeks, like she's flushed.

I pick up Grace and turn to look. Two trailers

down is a rusting, sagging silver Cadillac.

"Probably," I say. "This is the sort of place old Cadillacs go to die."

She walks toward it. "This is the first car I remember my father owning," she says.

I glance up at my parents' trailer. Nobody has noticed our arrival, so I follow her over to the car.

Arianna runs her hands along the side. "I remember it because I was finally big enough to open the door myself." Her fingers fit under the metal handle and she lifts.

It opens.

"Oh!" she says, surprised to see the door pop toward her. "It's not locked!"

"Nobody's going to steal it," I say. It probably doesn't even run.

She quickly closes the door, looking around anxiously. "I loved that car."

When no one comes outside, she peers into the backseat. "Oh, those seats! I used to get imprints on my legs from the seams."

She straightens. "I guess it's silly. I just didn't think I would ever see one again." Her hands smooth the skirt to her subdued slate blue dress. She has a simple cardigan on over it. She looks classy but not flashy. Her hair is a loose halo of curls today. It's perfect. She's perfect.

"Let's go up," I say. We dodge several overturned flower pots, their contents long ago spilled out, and head across the sparse dead grass to the deck of the trailer.

The steps are still solid. I bounce on each one to test its strength. From beneath the roof, I can see where the metal has pulled away from the boards. Easy fix. Just need a hammer and some fresh nails. Although screwing them in would be more sturdy.

I'm still assessing it when the screen door opens.

"There's that grandbaby!" Aunt Marge says. "Give that beautiful girl to me."

I pass Grace to Marge. Grace's baby hands immediately reach for the tufts of fuzzy orange hair Marge has pushed back with a headband.

We follow her into the house. It smells of cigarettes and lemon Pledge. The latter was probably hastily used this morning. The scarred coffee table has a shine to it. Probably Marge's idea. My mom never was much on housecleaning.

There's a couple afghans thrown over the sofa

and love seat that I don't recognize either. I'm guessing also Marge, trying to cover stains and cigarette burns.

It's hard to look at this place. I try to find some familiar comfort in it, but it's difficult. The carpet is rumpled and ragged. The striped wallpaper I remember so well is dingy, one big bright rectangle showing its original colors where a picture must have fallen recently.

It's so small and the ceiling is so low that I momentarily feel claustrophobic. I can't believe I lived here for eighteen years.

"Your mom is cooking up some eggs," Marge says. "Travis is out back with Donovan." She lifts Grace up in the air. "How is that perfect baby? We don't have near enough babies around here."

I glance over at Arianna, wondering how she's taking the place. Her eyes have fallen on a row of family pictures in cheap frames. She walks up to them. The first one shows my parents and me, still a baby. Dad has a mullet, which was a pretty good look for 1981. Mom's hair is big and puffed out. She's got bright green eyeshadow and a billion bracelets on her arm.

They're young, younger than I ever remember them being. I guess they were barely twenty when I was born. It's never struck me before how hard things must have been for them.

And they never got much better.

"I see Grace in you," Arianna says.

With that, Mom comes out of the kitchen, scooting past the dining table to walk up behind her. She's back in her signature tank top, even though it's November, and jeans that are ragged on the bottom.

"I saw it too, the minute I laid eyes on her," she says. "Same nose. Same expressions." She turns and grabs my ears. "Your ears changed, but they were just like your baby's when you were little."

She smells of coffee and cigarettes, but only faintly. Underneath is something familiar, a scent that is so basic, so intrinsic to who I am that I'm momentarily lost for words. It's the smell of her. My mother. My home.

I have to shake it off. My home is a penthouse in Manhattan. And that's when I'm not in Switzerland, where I have a chalet. Or LA, where I have a condo.

It's not here. Not in this seedy, rundown trailer with sagging walls and wrecked carpet.

I step back, unable to handle the proximity of the proof of where I came from. I spent thousands of dollars and a decade getting it behind me.

The back door slams, and Donovan and Travis trudge in, stomping their feet.

"Don't make a mess!" Marge admonishes them, but Mom just waves her hand.

"Don't worry about it. Bring a little of the outside in."

I remember her saying that when we were kids. My friends' moms had a fit if we had muddy feet or dirt on our jeans. Mom was chill. Her other favorite phrase was "A clean house is a sign of a wasted life."

Mom stays close, examining my face. "You look like something the cat drug in," she says. "You not used to late nights and drinking?"

I want to say I'm not used to secondhand smoke and cheap beer, but I bite it back. I can't find my rhythm here. Everything seems off kilter. "I'm past all that," I say.

"Uh-huh." She seems unconvinced.

A jingle draws our attention. In the corner, a tawny greyhound lifts her head. She's sleeping in an oversized dog bed.

"Who's this?" Arianna asks, heading for the dog.

"That's Take Your Bets," Mom answers. "She just retired last year. We call her Betsy."

"I heard you took in greyhound rescues," Arianna says. "We have one named Maximillion."

"Yes, sometimes we have two, but these days, it's just Betsy." She looks over at me. "Old Blue died a few years back."

I nod. We took in Old Blue a year before I left. He was a good one. They all were.

"Wynona, I think your eggs are burning," Marge says. She's still jiggling Grace, beaming at her like she's the princess of Birmingham.

"Oh, shit," Mom says, hurrying back to the kitchen.

"I told ya so," Uncle Travis says. He and Donovan have settled on the sofa.

Donovan takes out his wallet and passes Travis a five-dollar bill.

"What's this?" Marge asks.

Donovan shoves his wallet back in his jeans. "I bet Uncle Travis that Mom would actually succeed at cooking something this morning."

"Stupid bet!" Mom calls from the kitchen.

I take Arianna's hand. She's the only thing that makes sense to me right now, the grounding to my new life, not this old one that knocks me off center.

The smell of charred eggs blocks out all the others. I shake my head. Mom wasn't much of a cook either. She could make a mean Red Draw, though, beer and tomato juice. She had me drinking them from the age of sixteen. Now I cringe at a Bloody Mary. I take my alcohol straight.

Arianna and I squeeze past the Formica-topped table into the kitchen. Smoke rolls up from a pan on the stove. Mom turns off the burner.

"Well, damn it," Mom says. "I guess we'll be eating honey buns and grapes."

"It's fine," Arianna says.

"We got the good stuff still," she says, pouring orange juice from a pitcher into six glasses. She adds some grenadine to each glass. The drink turns red on the bottom, graduating up to dark orange and light orange on the top.

"How pretty," Arianna says as Mom hands her one. She takes a drink, then coughs, her hand coming to her mouth. "Oh, wow, what is it?"

"Tequila Sunrise," Mom says. "I might have gone

a little heavy on the tequila."

"It's ten in the morning!" I say.

"This is a breakfast drink!" she shoots back.

"Hand me one of those," Marge says, shifting Grace to her hip. "I do love a good Tequila Sunrise after a night of drinking."

Mom flashes me an "I told you so" look and hands a glass to her sister.

Arianna sips it again. "It is pretty good, once you know what you're drinking."

Mom laughs. "I think I like her better than you," she says to me. Then she grabs my head on both sides and drags it down so she can kiss my forehead. "You dumb lug. Spoilsport. My kid."

Donovan and Travis come into the kitchen to get their glasses. My brother passes one to me. "You can take the boy out of Alabama," he says, "but we can pour the Alabama right back in." He clinks my glass. "Chug-a-lug."

I sip the drink. It's not horrible, despite the cheap tequila.

We settle around the table. Mom has added a stool and a rocking chair so it can seat six. She dumps the burned eggs in the trash and plops a box of store-bought honey buns in the center of the table, each in its own shiny package.

Arianna sits close to me. "We should have stopped at a bakery on the way," she says.

I shrug. There's no telling what will delight or insult my family. Mom sets a bowl of grapes on the table.

This is where I come from. And navigating my time with them is just as bewildering to me now as it was thirteen years ago.

Chapter 18: Arianna

Dell is doing better with something concrete to do.

I sit on a lawn chair in the front yard, watching Dell and his brother fix the roof of the deck.

Wynona lies on a blanket on the ground, playing with Grace. Travis and Marge have left. We tried to convince Betsy to come out with us, but she refused to leave her dog bed.

We're all a little buzzed on Tequila Sunrises and I'm not sure power tools are the best idea at a time like this. But the boys seem to have the situation under control.

Everything is slower here. I thought Dell and I had taken things down a notch by going part-time, but there were always still a million things to attend to.

Not here.

Two boys, screwing down metal on a deck roof. A baby on a blanket.

Morning alcohol slowing down your blood.

I feel sleepy. It's not cold out, just the perfect amount of chilly air and warm sun. I don't spend a lot of time outside in New York. Being outdoors in Manhattan is deliberate. A walk in the park. An outdoor concert. Eating on a patio in Rockefeller Center.

Here, you just walk outside your own home, and sit.

"Should I mix up another batch?" Wynona asks, holding a colorful teething ring over Grace, who reaches with her chubby hands.

"Oh, no," I say. "I think we've had enough."

Wynona laughs. "We'll get you in shape to drink with the McDonalds." She picks up Grace and squishes her cheek against her. "I could just squeeze you forever."

I realize we don't have any pictures of Dell's

family in the penthouse. I need to fix that. This is Grace's grandmother, and she obviously dotes on her. There should be a record of it. Something for Grace to see between visits.

I tug my phone out of the hidden pocket of my skirt. "Let's get a shot of you two together," I say.

Wynona holds the pose, Grace against her.

"That's really good," I say, turning my phone to show her.

"Send it to me," she says. "Or to Byron, I guess. We only have one cell."

Dell looks up at the mention of his father's name. He's up on a ladder, holding the metal flat for Donovan to screw down.

"Just sending him a photo," I say.

Wynona rattles off his number, and I send the picture.

Of course, now Dell's father has my number. Maybe Dell can give his mother a phone for Christmas. I'm sure he'd rather I correspond with her, not his dad. I can send her images and updates about Grace.

I save the image to my favorites. Wynona settles back down with Grace, so I click over to Instagram to check on the whereabouts of my mother.

After our conversation about my engagement, she went to a bridal shop and began snapping mother-of-the-bride gowns. The comment reads "Guess why!"

Oh, Mother. She can't keep a secret for five seconds.

I'm planning to make a comment, but a notification pops up, and when I clear it, I realize the app uploaded my most recent image to my Instagram account. Whoa. Wait!

The pop-up was about the auto location tagging. So the new picture of Wynona and Grace not only posted, but it has a cute little link to the trailer park in Birmingham, Alabama.

Good thing I never use this account and no one follows me. I only have two pictures on it, both of food. The sole reason I have it at all is to check on Mom.

I navigate to the picture, looking for a way to delete it.

A phone rings inside the house.

"Let me get that," Wynona says, passing me the baby.

I take her, still trying to find a trash can or some other obvious way to delete the picture. Grace grabs the phone and shoves it in her mouth.

"Oh, baby, gross!" I say. I tug the phone away and wipe it on my skirt.

Grace howls, unhappy to lose the shiny toy. I reach down for a red and black caterpillar that squeaks or rattles or rustles, depending on which fat section of its body you squeeze.

She grabs it and sticks it in her mouth.

"You have more teeth coming in?" I ask her. She's facing away, so I can't really look.

Dell comes down the ladder. "All done," he says, giving the power drill a spin.

"Looks good," I say, shielding my eyes from the glare. The roof lies flat and straight over the deck.

Wynona comes out. "You got it?"

Donovan folds up the ladder. "All fixed. We should head to lunch."

Wynona nods. "That was Sara Lee, the assistant manager down at the track. She says Beck and Theresa want Hasmund to come to the race tonight. They have a spot in the Sky Box for you." She rolls her eyes. "Like the stands aren't good enough."

She elbows Donovan. "They said you could come too."

I look over at Dell. He shakes his head. "We need to pack up to leave," he says. I can see he doesn't want to risk any more exposure.

"You sure?" Donovan says. "Because I could use those contacts I might meet up in the box for the new job. Everything is who you know, not what you know."

Dell hesitates. I can see he's torn between helping his brother and breaking free of the family.

"The track people all seemed pretty nice," I say. I'm rooting for Donovan myself.

Dell looks from me to Donovan. "What about Grace? We can't take her into the club, and Mom's working."

"Marge can watch her," Wynona says quickly. "Grandma Jessie can help."

I try not to feel uneasy. This is Grace's family. I can't blow off their help without seeming like I don't trust them.

"I tell you what," Dell says. "Arianna and I will take Donovan there with us, stay about an hour, and leave you to wheel and deal." He claps his brother on the back. "That work?"

"Sounds great," he says. "Damn, how do I dress for that? Mom, you been up there?"

"I've seen 'em up there," she says. "Jeans and a button-down is good enough. You can throw on a sports coat if you like."

He nods. "All right. I got to take stock of what I brought." He heads inside.

"I'll help," Wynona says. She seems pleased to be useful.

She's not near as tough as she acts.

Grace drops her caterpillar. Dell picks it up and shakes off the dirt and dead grass. "Should I give it to her?" he says, inspecting it.

I laugh. "I think the expression you're looking for is 'Dirt don't hurt.'"

He shakes his head. "Our lives have definitely been short on practical euphemisms," he says.

"And tequila for breakfast," I add.

"And trailer parks."

I glance around. "There's definitely no trailer parks in Manhattan," I say. "Are they in New York?"

"Probably," he says. "I'm not up on my mobile real estate."

"Wait," I say. "Is that how Mobile, Alabama, got its name?"

He laughs so long my cheeks actually turn red.

"I guess not," I say.

"No, no, that's great," he says. "I love that idea. But if I remember my Alabama history correctly, it's just an Americanized version of the old French name. But it's a port city, so there's that."

"That makes sense," I say. Grace leans forward, and I have to hold her to keep her on my lap. "So when are we going to the track?"

"Saturday matinee is at two, but I figure they mean the evening post time at seven forty-five," he says. "You starving?"

"I've had grapes and tequila," I say. "Of course I'm starving."

He glances back at the door. "I say we fetch something more our style for lunch and bring it back. They can make fun of us if they want."

I nod.

Dell heads to the house. "I'll let them know what we're doing."

He goes in, the screen door banging behind him.

That's another thing. Screen doors. I've never

lived anywhere that didn't open into a hall. I'm not sure what they are even for. Air circulation? Why not just open the door?

With everyone inside, and the sounds of hammering and electric drills gone, the place is quiet. So quiet.

Way down the road, I hear a dog bark. A few birds twitter, the hardy ones who stay for winter, I guess. Although it doesn't really feel like winter. I'm sweating a little behind my knees.

Grace wants back on the blanket, so I let her down. She grabs a set of plastic baby keys and rolls on her back, staring at them.

Everything feels different here. New York must have seemed frantic and crowded to Dell when he arrived.

But he took to it like it was the land of his birth, as if the city was laid out just for him. And he owned some of it now, tall buildings that held more people than this trailer park plus all the blocks around it.

I wonder if he felt culture shock. If he had been lonely. If the move from Hasmund McDonald to Dell Brant had cost him anything.

And if leaving his family had been worth it.

Chapter 19: Dell

The racetrack seems no different from when I left. The big grandstand is the same, like wood blocks stacked together from the back side, all glass in the front.

The deep blue triangles of the rooftops complete the image that a child has haphazardly stacked her toys together.

It's night, so I can't make out all the details unless an area is lit up. The grass is green in a few spots, but mostly parched and dead. The driving range looks abandoned. Off to the side, the old horse barns look forlorn, only a few safety lights on the corners.

But the bushes are trimmed and the concrete paths have been power-washed. People mill around the outside waiting for the dogs to appear. Lots of people will follow their path from the paddock to the starting box.

"Where are we meeting them?" Arianna asks. She doesn't look around as much as I'd expect. She has been to a lot of horse tracks, owned by her parents' friends, so maybe they all seem the same to her.

"Someone will meet us in the Sky Club," I say. "It's partially open to spectators, but there are private rooms there as well."

Donovan tugs on his sports coat, looking around. "Man, I haven't been here in years," he says. "It was pretty depressing last time I saw it, but it looks like they've tried to spruce it up."

"Two-million-dollar renovation," I say. I'd seen the reports. I had not invested or been a part of it. Maybe I should have. Grudges. I needed to let them go.

My mother left hours ago to start her shift. She works on the ground floor, which is where the rowdy crowd hangs out at the bar and dance floor. She has stories about the terrible things she's seen and cleaned.

Dad will be off in the Greyhound Paddock. I don't expect to see him at all, although I assume Mom has told him we're here.

Walking up is another time warp for me during a weekend where I'd already had one too many stumbles down Memory Lane. I can picture all the places I used to go. My eyes roam beyond the public spaces, past locked chain-link gates to the paths behind the scenes. Very little has changed there, from what I can see.

We head inside and take escalators up to the sixth floor, the Sky Club level. At first I don't see anyone, but then a girl in a black dress approaches. "You must be the McDonalds." She glances at me. "You look like your dad."

Great.

"This way," she says.

I'm not terribly familiar with this floor. The only times I ever went here were when a trainer or owner asked me to go find somebody, as a young kid, in the early '90s before everyone had a cell phone to contact them on their own.

We follow the girl, someone in the role like

Armalina must have had long ago. Only now I'm the guy she leads around.

I'm no bigwig here. Just another McDonald, one who manages to dress a little better.

The Sky Club floor is open and dimly lit to avoid a reflection on the glass. We pass close to the front. The racetrack is bright outside, like day. A few people mill around, a photographer, waiting on the race, some personnel. At the end is the starting box. It has the gate with the individual spaces for each dog. It's surrounded with a tent. It's close to the first post time, so the lead-outs walk the dogs along the path to place them in the gate.

I should keep going, but I pause to look at the lead-outs. A few of them are young, but overall they are older, trainers, maybe. I suppose the system has changed over time. It occurs to me that this is a goal that I will never reach. I will never walk a greyhound from the ginny pit to the gate.

"You coming?" Arianna asks. She looks anxious now. She knows I'm acting out of character.

I nod and press on. Donovan chats up the cute girl leading us as we go through a door. She seems into him, smiling and fiddling with her hair.

Inside is a big room with a fair number of spectators, all laughing and drinking, paying no mind to the races.

But we pass through it.

"This way," the girl says.

Another door. The new area is much smaller. Only a few people sit around tables covered in cloth. There are complimentary tip sheets and private betting machines.

Beck stands. "Glad to see you could make it," he says, extending a hand. I shake it, then he moves on to Donovan. When Arianna extends hers, Beck lightly kisses the back of it. She flushes.

I'm not sure why Beck wants us here. We settle at a table next to his. His wife Theresa gives a wave, then turns her attention back to the track.

"Send the waitress," Beck says to the girl who brought us, and she nods.

"Post time," Theresa says.

I glance at the giant board that lists the stats for the race. Betting odds. The amount of money that's been put on the dogs. There's a clear favorite, but one thing I know about greyhounds is that they can be unpredictable.

The mechanical rabbit zooms along the rail, and then the gun fires.

The gate opens and eight greyhounds race out.

The pack splits quickly between three leaders and the laggards. The dogs are a blur at first, but as they round the second turn, they begin to slow enough that you can make out the numbers on their colored jerseys.

Arianna rises, stepping closer to the window. "I've only been to horse races," she says.

Beck stands beside her, lifting his own gleaming binoculars from the table. "Use these," he says. "It's fascinating to look at them up close."

She brings them to her eyes, her head turning as she follows their path. "They're wearing muzzles!" she exclaims. "Like little cages!"

"They can get nippy," Beck says. "This protects them from each other."

Another couple enters the room, and Beck goes to greet them. Donovan perks up. He's anxious to meet and greet. It's a good sign that he will do well in business.

I enjoy watching Arianna get so involved in the race. The first greyhound crosses, then the next and the next. She brings down the binoculars, staring at the finals listed on the board.

"Somebody won some money," she says. "Number six had long odds."

Beck comes back around. "Feel free to bet if you like. On the house."

Beck introduces the couple, a pair in their sixties, jovial and friendly. I nod politely and let Donovan do the talking. It's interesting to be no one after years as Dell Brant.

Arianna sits next to me again. "This is so different from horses," she says.

"Agreed," I say. The results go final on the board, and after a moment, the stats move to race two. "Did you want to bet?"

"Sure," she says, sliding the tip sheet toward her. "Which name do you like better, LadyBeFirst or ShiftyButQuick?" She frowns. "I think I'd choose a lady before shifty."

"That's a terrible way to choose," I say with a laugh. "But I'll take Shifty. See who everyone is betting on."

She studies the boards and reads through the dogs' statistics. Beck sits beside her and begins to school her on how the dogs' odds are assessed and how they adjust based on the bets.

I watch the next set of lead-outs bring the dogs forward, my gut tensing. This set is younger, like it used to be. The bugle sounds, alerting everyone that post time is approaching.

The patrol judge and the paddock judge wait near one end of the track. Each dog steps on a scale and the paddock judge notes its weight. A couple of dogs pee on the side before jumping on, part of their training.

They all pass and the lead-outs move toward the center line, dogs close at hand. The judge checks all the muzzles, making sure each dog is secure. They line up to be examined by the crowd placing their bets.

The announcer breaks in, talking briefly about each dog, urging people to place their bets in the last few minutes before post time.

"Is it like horse racing," Arianna asks, leaning in close, "where the ones that pee before they run do better?"

I grin. "Not sure that holds true with dogs. You going to bet?"

She nods. I move to go with her to the machine,

but Beck takes over. I sit back. When I worked here, employees weren't allowed to bet, even if you were old enough, but some of the workers had friends place bets for them.

At the time, I couldn't see throwing any of my hard-earned money away. I'd need it when I left.

I'd still never placed a bet on an animal. Start-ups, sure. Ailing companies I thought I could resurrect or sell for profit, definitely. But not dogs or horses.

I don't think that part of me has changed.

People like to talk about the mistreatment of the greyhounds and want to end the racing. It has definitely happened. But I haven't seen it much. A few doctored dogs, swiftly handled, usually privately, banned from racing. A couple who were mistreated, trainers who were also not allowed to come back.

Maybe other tracks weren't as careful. I wouldn't have stood for anybody hurting a dog, had I seen it. But mainly I was only around the empty kennels, washing down the concrete floors.

Arianna returns to her seat, holding her betting receipts.

"Who did you choose?" I ask.

"I did Lady to win, Swifty to show," she says.

"Long odds on Lady," I point out.

"I'm a risk-taker with other people's money." She laughs and leans into me.

The lead-outs move their dogs back toward the starting box. I swallow again as they load them in. If we were outside, near them, we'd hear the barking and excited sounds of them entering the metal gates.

I remember standing nearby, my broom propped beside me on the fence. I memorized every movement of the lead-outs, how they held the leashes, the happy yelps of the dogs.

Arianna picks up the binoculars, one hand gripping my arm. She's excited now, and this makes me happy. I like seeing her have fun.

One dog balks in the gate, and the announcer makes note of the number. Bets are frozen as the post time clock runs out.

A moment passes, then the rabbit runs down the rail again.

And they are off.

Arianna jumps up, so much more animated now that there is money riding on her choices. She looks through the binoculars, then brings them down, then back up.

I stand beside her. Beck smiles. "It's fun to watch their first time," he says.

Another couple enters. Donovan moves behind us, eager to meet the new arrivals. I stand close to Arianna.

"It's so fast," she says.

Lady is in the middle of the pack, but Swifty has pulled ahead. I glance at his odds. Two to one. Not a big payout on a bet to show. But still, it's amusing.

He crosses the line and Arianna jumps in the air. "Look at Swifty!" she says. The last dog crosses, Lady still mid-pack.

"That was amazing!" she says. "I never bet at the horse races. I only went with my parents, and my mother thought betting was too *bourgeois*."

I laugh. "She might be right."

The door opens again. I don't bother to look. I'm not sure why we're here, really, unless Beck has some sort of surprise. I try to stay calm about someone who might know me as Dell. I can't imagine it would happen here in Birmingham, but this Sky Box increases the odds over the trailer park.

Arianna studies the tip sheet for race three. "I like the looks of this one," she says. "Run4theMoney."

She looks up at me, then behind me, and she freezes. "Oh my God," she says, and drops the tip sheet.

"What is it?" I ask, turning.

An elegant woman with sleek ash blond hair has arrived, along with a distinguished man in his late fifties. They stand out in the room, New York written all over them among the southerners.

Arianna grips my hand. "Those are my parents."

Chapter 20: Arianna

What are my parents doing here?

I feel hot and sick and scared and freaked out.

They will call him Dell!

Beck knows him as Hasmund!

So does Donovan!

They all think the baby belongs to both of us!

Mom knows I was never pregnant!

Everything is about to blow up in our faces.

Dell grabs my hand. "It will be all right," he says.

"No, it won't!" I hiss.

"Arianna!" my mother says, walking toward me, arms outstretched. She looks like she just came off a runway in a sleek heather gray sheath and killer stilettos. Her hair is perfectly coiffed in a long bob. Chunky jewelry on her neck, wrists, and ears could only have been put together by a stylist.

"What do we do?" I whisper in Dell's ear.

"Just fake it," Dell says.

"Darling," Mom says, leaning forward as if she'll hug me, but I know better. That would muss her hair. She air-kisses me instead. Can't wreck the lipstick.

She holds my shoulders as she takes in my blue dress and cardigan. Off the rack. Knockoff. Not her standard.

"You look like you're fitting in here," she says.

That's about the best she can do without insulting me.

She turns to Dell. "And please introduce us."

Oh, God. How do I do this?

But Dell extends a hand. "I'm pleased to meet you, Mrs. Hart," he says, avoiding his name. "Arianna speaks so well of you."

"Bridget, please," Mom says, watching him with hooded eyes. "I was delighted to hear of your engagement to my daughter."

"Hey, princess," Dad says, giving me a proper

hug. "Mom saw that picture you posted and realized you were in Alabama. She practically lassoed a plane to get here."

"Thank goodness we could make it," Mom says. Her eyes flit between me and Dell. "Who was the woman in the image? A babysitter, perhaps?"

Shit shit shit. I stumble, but it's Beck who saves us this time.

He walks up, extending his hand to Dad as he says, "When I got the call, I could scarcely believe we'd have Cambridge Hart here at our track."

Theresa comes forward to clasp Mom's hand. "We arranged for the happy couple to be here as well. You must be so thrilled. We couldn't get enough of these two at the engagement party last night."

My mother sends me a side glance. "How lovely for Dell's family to offer a party. I wish we could have come."

Theresa tilts her head at the word "Dell."

I stifle my gasp, my fingers in a death grip on Dell.

He smooths past it with a change of subject. "Please sit near us," he says to Mom, pulling out a chair.

This breaks up the little party. I notice Donovan near the side wall, stars in his eyes with the presence of my parents. Yeah, they're probably good contacts to have.

My heart will not stop hammering. This cannot possibly end well.

I tell myself it's Dell's secret, the name part. That I shouldn't worry. But it's Grace too. And she is mine, even if it isn't on paper yet. The Duchess can't be involved. No one can know.

My palms start to sweat.

Each table seats four, so Dell and I sit with my parents.

Theresa and Beck want to hover, I can tell, but they are polite and retreat to their original seats.

The room is a little fuller now with the other couples. Donovan approaches and I don't see how we can introduce him without messing up the name again.

But Dell has it well in hand. "This is my brother Donovan," he says. "He just graduated from the University of Texas in International Business. I think we can all agree that Alabama is like a whole 'nother country."

Everyone laughs. Donovan pulls up a chair, and I lean into Dell.

His face is relaxed, attentive, calm. But I can sense the underlying tension in his body.

Mom turns to me. "So tell me about this party last night." Like Dell, her face is placid and pleasant. But I can see the falseness in her smile.

"It was a surprise," I say. "We came down for a nice luncheon with family, but they planned an impromptu event."

Dell squeezes my hand, and I know I've done well. I can avoid names. Skirt issues.

It's just that she's my mother. In the end I will probably do no better avoiding what she wants than Dell did for this morning's breakfast.

Donovan looks at each of us, smoothing his hand along his jaw. He's picking up on the redirects, the feints.

"Where do you all hang your hat?" he asks my parents.

"Spoken like a born-again Texan," Dell says. Everyone laughs.

My father answers him. "We are based out of New York, like Dell and Arianna here."

Donovan's face flickers at the second mention of this name. "My brother took his sweet time making it back to Alabama," Donovan says. He's not saying Dell's name either. He's bound to be figuring it out. "But I've been in Texas for years myself. I appreciate them coming down while I was visiting. How long are you here for?"

"I'm sure we'll all head back tomorrow," Dell says. "Arianna and I are expected in the office. Won't you come with us?" he asks my parents.

And this is when my show-off attitude from a few days ago bites me in the butt.

"Do you have your private plane here?" Mom asks.

You could have heard a pin drop in the Sky Box.

Donovan speaks first. "You have your own plane, brother?"

"Well, how 'bout that," Beck says, leaning back in his chair so he can get a better look. "Now that's a showboat if I ever heard of one."

"Must be mighty convenient," Theresa says. "Beck and I dread flying anywhere."

"I do have it here," Dell says evenly. "I can send a driver after you in the morning if you'd like to go back with us."

Mom glances over at Dad with a knowing nod. She seems pleased.

"Your plane rated for that many people?" Dad asks. "My friend Frank Marker can only carry four plus a pilot."

"It's a jet," Dell says simply. "And I can carry ten plus crew."

The room goes quiet, probably everyone thinking about what it must be like to have your own private plane. Thankfully, the gun fires for the next race, and the rest of the room turns to the windows to watch the greyhounds.

"All right, darling," Mom says. "We can catch up with details on the flight." She glances around. "This is quite a large facility."

Beck leans over again, his hand on the back of my chair. "One of the largest. Opened in 1987. Had its doom-and-gloom years, but we just finished a major renovation."

"Same ownership all this time?" my father asks, and I don't miss my mother's subtle elbow in his gut.

I'm sweating everywhere. I hadn't corrected my mother's belief that Dell's family owned the racecourse. I had no idea this was going to happen.

Beck handles it. "Oh, no. It's changed hands a few times. Right now it's a fellow out of Montgomery. We don't see him much. I've been managing it for a couple decades."

Mom nods politely, but I can see wheels turning, trying to figure out Dell's family's position here if not the owner or manager. She turns to Dell. "I'm surprised your family isn't up here in the box."

Beck raises his eyebrows at that.

"Oh, they're around," Dell says.

"We should meet them!" Mom says. "Is there another club level?"

I can hear in her voice that she hopes so. This one hasn't impressed her.

"They have a lot of duties on race night," Dell says. He glances at me. "Your arrival is quite the surprise. We hadn't planned on seeing my parents tonight."

I'm panicking. She's my mother, but her superpower is the ability to judge people and dismiss them faster than traffic court.

I'm in no way ready to have her meet Wynona and, God, Byron. The father who thinks I'm stout.

Who nearly came to blows with Dell last night.

This is an unmitigated disaster. The only thing I can hope for is a cyclone to swoop in and take all of Birmingham Race Course with it.

Chapter 21: Dell

Arianna is starting to lose it. Her breath is speeding up.

"I'm sure your parents can spare a minute," Bridget says. She's suspicious and more than a little cool. The exact opposite of her warm, friendly daughter. I'm used to women like Bridget, society types. It's what makes Arianna so special, that she can come from a life like that and be as wonderful as she is.

"Relax and take a breather," Cambridge says, pressing his hand on his wife's thigh. "We just got here."

Bridget relents for the moment, settling back in her seat.

The race outside has ended, and the chatter starts up again, laughter and the tinkling of glasses.

A waitress comes by to ask if we would like drinks. I have every intention of keeping a clear head. But Arianna orders tequila, straight, so I order the same to avoid her looking out of place.

Bridget raises an eyebrow and declines a drink.

Beck turns to us again. "How did your dog run in the last race?" he asks Arianna.

She hasn't paid any attention to the results. "I don't think I remembered to place a bet," she says.

"Let's figure out a winner for you in the next one," he says. "One for you and one for mom." He's angling to curry favor, but I can tell from a hundred paces that gambling is not Bridget's thing. He should back off.

But if Arianna's mother is good at anything, it's keeping up civil appearances. She fakes interest in the tip sheet and allows Beck to run the machine for her. She doesn't even glance at the betting receipt when he lays it on the table in front of her like an offering to a queen.

The drinks come and Arianna downs hers straight, earning her another disapproving glance from her mother.

So I do what any self-respecting future husband would do, and that's down my own shot and look curiously at Bridget, saying, "I guess you're not much for flattering the locals."

Bridget sits tall, shocked to be caught doing something that could be considered ungracious. When the girl comes to take our empties, she says, "I'd love to try one of those."

Arianna squeezes my hand. She knows tequila is not native or particularly important to Alabama culture. And that my family is not necessarily a representative sample of Birmingham's population. But we're in this together.

"Are you sure we can't just pop in to say hello to Dell's family?" Bridget asks Arianna. "If not the father, then surely the mother. Can you ring them, perhaps? Let them know where we are?"

"Mom doesn't keep a phone on her," I say. "She enjoys being off grid."

"I'd do it if I could," Cambridge says. "I feel tied to the damn thing." He tugs out his phone and sets it on the table.

Beck clears his throat. "I'll send someone to fetch her," he says. He waves over the girl who met us at the escalators.

My brother leans in. "You sure you want to let him do that?" he asks me. "Mom is not a fan of Beck."

I'm not sure of anything.

"Why don't we arrange a nice breakfast tomorrow?" I ask Bridget. "Away from the track. You two must be exhausted from the travel."

"I'd love to get their perspective on the facility," Bridget insists. "How long has your family been involved in racing?"

"Since before I was born," I say.

Beck claps me on the back. "This little guy used to shadow his father. He loved the dogs when they arrived in '92. Perfect work for a young man."

"We had horses before," Theresa adds. She is eager to get back into a conversation with Arianna's parents. "Tried them again a few years back, but the business has changed a lot."

Bridget doesn't react to any of this, just watching one person, then the other. She's a hard nut to crack.

"Mom," Arianna says, "I really think it's best we do something tomorrow. We didn't plan for you two to be here. You could have let me know."

Bridget waves her hand to dismiss her daughter's complaint. "I've already realized I needed to take the bull by the horns if I was going to get anywhere with you. You've been too secretive lately." She glances around. "I assume someone is keeping the baby?"

"Oh, she is a precious little girl," Theresa says. "Life of the party last night."

This conversation can't go on another minute. We need to take Arianna's family aside about Grace, and this is not the place to do it.

"That reminds us," I say swiftly. "We have been definitely intruding on Marge's time." I turn to Bridget. "My aunt is watching Grace. We should get back to her."

"Oh no, Hasmund," Theresa says. "The baby is surely sleeping by now. Enjoy yourselves."

And there it is. My old name.

Bridget stares pointedly at the woman. "What did you call him?"

"Hasmund," Theresa says, uncomfortable under the other woman's glare. "We aren't very formal here." She glances at her husband uncertainly. "But if Mr. McDonald is more appropriate…"

Her voice trails off. Everyone is quiet.

Well, hell. We really could have stood to have prepped Arianna's parents on this too.

Bridget flattens her hands on the table. "Will someone kindly explain to me what is going on? Why can't we see the Brants? And why is everyone calling Dell by this other name?"

I'm about to come up with a workable lie, when my brother leans into Bridget, as if telling her a secret.

"My brother here never really liked his given name," Donovan says. "He hasn't used it since he was a teen. Everyone used to tease him."

Saved by the brother. I shrug like it's all no big deal. "I'm known professionally as Dell," I say.

Arianna clenches my hand like she's going underwater. "Mom, we're leaving. You can stay if you like." She gestures to Theresa and Beck. "You have great hosts."

Dang, Arianna is taking a chance, leaving her parents with people who have a different story about Grace. But I help her double down.

"Or you can ride with us," I say. "We can take

you where you are staying, perhaps have a drink downtown. I can show you my home city."

Before Bridget can respond, Arianna stands up. I move with her. Donovan stands also. The Harts have to come to their feet or look impolite.

"All right, Arianna," Bridget says. "We'll play along."

Beck and Theresa scramble from their chairs.

"So glad you could make it out," Theresa says.

Beck comes up to shake Cambridge's hand. "Sure wish you could hang around a spell."

"Next time," he says. "I'm sure we'll be back."

I hope not. Not here, anyway. I place my hand on the back of Arianna's waist to lead her out.

The next room is raucous and loud. Bridget has to arrange her expression carefully to avoid telegraphing her displeasure.

The main club space is more spread out and quieter.

Arianna leans in. "What are the odds we'll run into your mother on the way down?"

"Low," I assure her. "She clears tables on the bottom floor, which is a nightclub. It's crowded and loud and rowdy. We'll avoid it."

We head for the escalators. Bridget keeps her arms close to her body, clutching a designer purse as if she might get soiled by the unwashed masses.

Our little party goes down one set of escalators, then two.

And it happens.

As we go down, my father passes us, going up. He's sweaty and somewhat grimy, hoisting a case of hamburger buns on his shoulder. He runs supplies for the concessions during the busy times.

His face whips around, taking in me, then Arianna, and visibly reacting to the Harts. They definitely don't look like they're from around here.

We keep descending, but he shouts, "Hasmund, you wait right there."

I'm not sure what to do, ignore him or comply. Damn rotten luck.

"Who is that?" Bridget asks.

I find it best not to answer, as both a lie and the truth are problematic.

We make it to the next landing and are headed toward the mouth of the next escalator when we hear a THUNK.

Dad has dropped the plastic tray holding the

buns on the floor and races down the escalator, skipping stairs.

Now I know exactly how Arianna must have felt when she saw her family. I turn to Donovan. "Might as well go find Mom. This is about to get interesting."

Donovan takes off down the escalators.

We wait for Dad to arrive. Bridget's hand is on her chest. Cambridge looks amused. Arianna has a death grip on my hand.

Here we go.

Chapter 22: Arianna

I'm not thrilled to be face to face with this man again.

Dell's father takes the escalator two and three steps at a time. He stops short in front of Dell. "What the hell are you doing here?"

"Beck asked me to be his guest," he says easily.

"It's not going to do you any good to hobnob with the management," Byron says. "You trying to sell him some computers?"

Dell shakes his head. "Why would I do that?"

I want to reach out a hand, try to fix that misconception I gave him at the party last night, but then I realize — it doesn't matter. Among the issues we're about to have, Dell's job description is super low in priority.

Mom draws a breath, as if to correct this incorrigible man on the error of his accusations, but then she holds it in.

I figure she's seen it. The resemblance. It's striking. Even with Byron's hair slicked down from work and the dirty work pants and the rolled-up sleeves, you see it.

"Who is this?" Mom manages to ask. "Another brother?"

Only I can feel the tension in Dell as he says, "No, this is my father, Byron."

Byron looks Mom in the eye, then rakes his gaze down her sheath dress. I cringe, waiting for him to say something barbaric.

My own dad is the first to recover. "We're about to be related," he says, extending a hand. "I'm Arianna's father, Cambridge Hart."

The two men shake.

Then my dad surprises me. He pulls out a cigar case from his breast pocket. He doesn't smoke, so I'm as shocked as anyone to see it. He opens the case and shows it to Dell's father, three Cuban cigars, lined up in a perfect row.

"Finest illegal import you can find. Snuck it in on my flight this morning. Do you smoke?"

"I'll smoke one of those," Byron says.

I think both my mom and I wince as Byron reaches into the case with smudged hands. Dad takes one for himself and withdraws a finely crafted cutter to snip off the ends.

"Where might a man light up one of these without pissing off a security guard?" Dad asks.

Byron turns to the escalators. "I'll show you." He nods at Dell a moment, drags his gaze across my mother a second time, and they are off.

"Well, I'll be," Bridget says. "My husband is smoking and cussing like a commoner."

"Oh, Mom," I say. "You sound like an eighteenth-century monarch."

"It's just so out of character," she says, taking my arm. "Take me someplace less horrible to wait for him, and explain to me what Dell's father does at this track. He appears to follow the belief that he should not ask his employees to do what he himself will not."

"This way," Dell says.

I try to read him as we head back up the escalator. His stance is relaxed, but his hands are tight. This can't be easy for him. An entire adulthood of avoiding his past, just to have it blast right back at him.

But these are his parents. We can't keep them from mine. If anyone should know, it has to be my family. They were going to meet at the wedding anyway. Might as well hash all this out now.

Unless we elope.

Our little party of three passes the tray of buns that Byron dropped to the floor, and Dell picks it up. He places them on a table.

We cross the mostly empty room. There's a restaurant here. Race fans sit at tables filled with food. The announcer is piped in, small televisions at every table.

Dell flags a waitress and speaks to her quietly. He's trademark Dell now, charming and self-assured. It helps, I'm sure, that we don't have anyone near us who can upset my mother. But there is no telling what Byron is saying to Dad.

The possibilities are horrible.

The waitress takes us to a table in a far corner,

away from the main walkways. The view of the track is minimal, but that suits my mother anyway. She is not the least bit interested in the dogs.

We're handed menus. "I'll be back," the waitress says.

My mother immediately sets hers down, folding her hands into her lap. "Is anyone going to inform me what's going on?"

Dell and I exchange glances. She's my mother. But it's his secret.

"Why does it matter what Dell's family does here?" I ask. "Or that he goes by a different name?"

"I feel left out of the equation, Arianna," Mom says stiffly. "What else are you hiding?"

Dell places the menu carefully on the table. "Bridget, my parents have worked at this racecourse since before I was born. My father assists in the upkeep of the animals' quarters and helps in concessions on race days. My mother is downstairs in the nightclub, clearing tables."

For a moment, my mother does not speak. She takes in the table, the room, the glass wall to the track beyond.

"Thank you for finally playing it straight with

me," she says. She plucks at her bracelets, tidying them up so the beads align. I've never seen her like that, avoiding eye contact. Normally she sits still and levels people with her stare.

"May I ask why you have not elevated your family's circumstances, given you flew here on your own jet?" she asks. Her eyes flicker to my face, but she does not look at Dell.

"They like their life," he says. "It's good, honest work. They have what they need and want."

"What of your brother?" she asks.

"He finished college. He has a job. I'll assist where I am able."

She takes in a deep breath. "So your name is — what did she say — Hasbro?"

"Hasmund," Dell says. "I changed it after I graduated."

"Well, I agree with that decision," she says. "It doesn't suit you."

"The change is not commonly known," he says. "I didn't want a connection to it."

Now she sits up straighter. "You should not be ashamed of your roots, Dell. Nor your family." She turns to me now. "And you should not keep secrets from your parents."

Dell and I catch each other's gaze across the table. I know he's thinking about Grace, and the Duchess.

"Then let's be clear about Grace," Dell says. "She is biologically mine, and Arianna is in the process of adopting her. Because we will shortly have a new birth certificate that lists Arianna, we have kept things simple and allowed Arianna to step in as the mother."

Now my mother's gaze is sharp. "And who is the real mother?"

"I am the real mother," I say, my voice as cutting as her expression. "Her birth mother did not wish to raise her and has asked me to do it."

She turns to Dell. "Are the legalities in order?"

"They will be," he says. "The baby was born overseas, so there are international laws to navigate."

She sighs. "Arianna, what have you gotten yourself mixed up in?"

Now my anger starts to surface. "A life, Mother," I say. "A life with a child I adore and a man I love." I gesture to Dell. "I can't imagine that you don't admire him! He's just the sort of husband you'd dream up for me!"

The waitress returns, sees our strained faces, and takes off again.

"He's fine, Arianna, and I'm delighted you've settled down," she says. "I just don't understand the subterfuge. Your father and I have always lived life very openly."

"Of course," I say. "It's easy when you come from a long line of rich people getting richer."

"Wealth is not at issue," she says. "Come now, perhaps you should order another tequila." She wrinkles her nose. "I had no idea it was popular here. Wikipedia says there is a drink called the 'Alabama Slammer.'" She looks at me pointedly. "I did do my homework and I pride myself on not offending the people of the places I visit."

Dell coughs into his hand, trying to control a laugh.

"Oh, Mom," I say. "You really are more suited for Paris."

The waitress peeks around the wall at us. "Did I hear someone say they would like an Alabama Slammer?" she says.

"A pitcher," Dell says. "Might as well do it right."

The waitress nods.

He picks up a menu. "We might want to order some food if we're drinking again tonight."

I've never had the drink he just ordered. But I could definitely use something before Dad comes back with Byron. Or Donovan with their mother.

Just picturing my sleek socialite mother with tattooed, smoking, cussing Wynona makes something called an Alabama Slammer sound like the perfect thing.

Chapter 23: Dell

The pitcher arrives with three glasses and I order things that I'm sure Arianna's mother doesn't normally touch. Tater tots. Fried mushrooms. I throw in some bread. We'll want this train wreck of a drink to get absorbed by something.

I pour the Alabama Slammers.

Bridget lifts the glass and takes a tentative sip. She smiles politely and sets it down again.

I haven't drunk liquor this cheap since, well, okay, since this morning. Alabama Slammers were a fixture of my youth, a mix of various types of alcohol and orange juice.

From the corner of my eye, I see Donovan weaving through the tables. Hell, I've forgotten he was fetching my mother. We're pretty hidden back here and she may not be able to get away for long.

I stand and wave at him. When I sit down, I quickly tell Bridget, "My mother and brother are not aware that the baby is not biologically Arianna's. We haven't had time to sit with them about it."

"This seems like the perfect moment," she says.

Blast it all. We have no intention of saying otherwise. This is unraveling fast.

"Mom, no," Arianna says firmly. "We have told you these things in confidence. Now is not the time."

Donovan strolls through the tables, confident and friendly now that he knows where he's headed. Most of the women take notice of him. He's a natural flirt, stopping by and saying hello, whether they are sitting with a date or not.

Mom is behind him, looking weary and more than a little pissed off. She spies us at the table.

"You get kicked out of the Sky Box?" she asks. "I could have told you those people were too full of themselves to be around a normal person." She stops when she sees Bridget. "Who's this?"

I stand. "Mom, this is Bridget Hart, Arianna's mother. They flew in this afternoon to congratulate us on the engagement. Bridget, this is Wynona."

"Well, shit," Mom says. "Why didn't they come in last night so they could have been at the party?"

"It was a surprise," I remind her. "You didn't bother to tell us either."

"Damn it all," she says. "If I knew they could've come out, I would have told them."

The two women do not shake hands. Mom stands uncertainly by Donovan on the far side of the table. Bridget remains seated. Her graciousness seems to be wearing thin.

Mom glances around. "I'm supposed to be on shift," she says. "The empties pile up and there's not enough highball glasses to go around."

"I'll message Beck, tell him to let you off tonight," I say. I can pull that string in a heartbeat.

"Beck's not my boss," she says.

"Beck is your boss's boss," I say.

"You trying to get me fired?" she shoots back.

"You've worked here for forty years," I tell her. "No one is going to fire you."

"You haven't met that twit who manages the

crew now. Twenty-five and thinks she knows everything." Mom's hands go to her hips, elbows out. She's brewing for a fight.

"Mom, sit down for a second," Donovan says. He pulls out a chair for her.

She fusses with the apron around her waist. I realize she hasn't said a single thing directly to Arianna's mom.

Bridget has also gone unnaturally quiet.

I'm not sure how to bridge the gap between them.

The waitress brings the appetizers. The girl spots Donovan and her hip juts out a little. She pops a piece of pink bubble gum in her mouth and swings her ponytail. "Hey, haven't seen you here in a while."

"Been gone a while," he says.

Mom pushes the plate away. "That bread only costs them ten cents and they charge four bucks for it. That's a crime if you ask me."

The waitress raises her eyebrows. "Don't you work on the ground floor?"

Now my anger is starting to peak. "She's with us for the moment," I say firmly.

The waitress lets out a little huff, looking at

Donovan as if he will defend her honor.

"She's my mother too," he says. "And Dell here is friends with Beck."

"Shit," the girl murmurs. "Sorry." She backs away.

"Bring us some of those onion tanglers," Mom says after her. "And you can forget your tip."

She picks up a piece of the overpriced bread and takes Donovan's silverware. "I haven't ever eaten up here," she says, opening a foil-wrapped square of butter and spreading it over the bread.

"Dad is with Arianna's father," I say to Mom. "We saw him on the escalators."

"He's inside?" She looks around, bread in her hand. "I guess they didn't need him out with the dogs."

Bridget turns to Arianna. "This was the woman in the picture you posted," she says. "Was that the baby?"

Now Mom's eyes light up. "Sweetest little girl in the whole world. Cute as a button and good as can be. Didn't cry all day."

"You spent the day with her?" Bridget asks. I think I catch a bit of jealousy in her tone.

"Yup, since breakfast." Mom sets the bread on a plate. "Made a day of it. Donovan and Dell fixed the roof of the deck. And your daughter and I sat with the baby outside. It was a nice day for it."

Bridget turns to Arianna with something akin to amazement. "Just a quiet day," she says.

Arianna shrugs. "The weather is mild here for November."

Bridget sits up a little straighter. "When do I get to see this baby?" she asks.

Mom's face whips around to Arianna. "Your mama hasn't met your baby?"

I jump in to save her. "This was your first weekend too," I say. "We're a busy couple with rather difficult jobs."

"But that's your mama," Mom says, waving the knife between Bridget and Arianna. She's adding butter to the bread. "She should have been up there when you were in labor. Helped out in those hard first weeks." She sets the knife down. "Were you even there when she was born?"

Now Bridget is angry. "That child isn't even hers."

Arianna gasps. "Mom!"

Damn it all. This will take some cleaning up.

But my mom is chill. She takes a bite of bread. "Now that's where you're wrong. I never saw a mother more devoted to her child." She chews, almost daring anyone to question her manners. "Though I'm wondering where she got it from."

Bridget sucks in a breath. She turns to Arianna. "I think I've had quite enough."

She tries to stand, but Arianna's hand shoots out. "Sit, Mother. We don't even know where Dad is."

Bridget lowers herself slowly back into the chair. "I didn't come here to be insulted."

"Seems like someone is just speaking truth around here," Mom says.

She is on a roll. I'm not sure whether to stop her or let it play out. I know how Arianna feels about her mother. Arianna loves her, but all the choices she's made for her entire life stem from this one betrayal. Her mother leaving her to be raised by nannies.

Bridget turns to her daughter. "Have you told this woman things?" she asks. "About how we traveled? You know I only did it for all those wonderful charities that needed leading."

Mom reaches for another piece of bread and

carefully opens another foil butter. She no longer seems to care about missing her shift.

Donovan's eyebrows are permanently glued in the lifted position. He catches my gaze, and his eyes widen.

"I did not say a word," Arianna says. "Maybe it's just plain that you were never around."

Bridget brings her hand to her throat.

"I thought so," Mom says. "Arianna, just let it out. Tell your mother how you feel."

"You did leave me," Arianna says, her voice breaking.

I wish her mother wasn't between us. I can't reach her hand to hold it.

Bridget draws in a breath. "But Arianna, that baby isn't yours. You would have told me if you were pregnant. You said you're adopting it."

Mom shrugs at this comment, as if it is immaterial that the baby wasn't born to Arianna now that we've gotten to the good stuff.

"I am," Arianna says, realizing the lie is no longer necessary. "And I'm there for her. I'm not putting other things first. Dell and I have both gone part-time."

Mom does cut in at this. "Who is Dell?"

Donovan stills her hands, buttering the bread so heavily that it appears frosted. "Hasmund goes professionally by another name," he says.

Mom drops the bread entirely. "Is the name I chose for you not good enough? Are the McDonalds not good enough for you?"

Now Bridget seems pleased. "He goes by Dell Brant," she says. "No one even knows the other name. He's quite well off, you know." Her face seems smug. "Funny that he has left you and your husband to toil at such low-level jobs while he has a plane and a penthouse."

She's gone too far. Mom switches from being upset at me to severely pissed off at her. "Byron and I don't need any handouts, not from family or nobody. We live perfectly fine." She stands up, tightening her apron. "Now if you'll excuse me, I have a job to do."

Donovan and I stand too.

"Mom," Donovan says, "Arianna and Hasmund are getting married. You need to find common ground with her family."

"Ah, baloney," she says. "They'll go off and do their jet-setting life, and leave the hard work to the kids to raise the babies. It's obvious they don't get their hands dirty."

She stalks off for the elevator. Donovan follows her, but I'm not sure what to do. Arianna is still sitting, her head in her hands. Bridget waits stiffly beside her.

"I'd like it very much if someone would fetch my husband," Bridget says. "I'm quite through with Birmingham, Alabama." She picks up her drink. "And this cocktail is atrocious."

Arianna texts her father as I look around the restaurant. I'm not sure this could have gone any worse.

Chapter 24: Arianna

That definitely could not have gone any worse.

When Dad and Byron return, they seem to have hit it off. After Byron leaves for his duties, Dad says Byron is "a little rough around the edges" but seems like a good hardworking man who is very proud of his sons.

Dell doesn't respond to that. I know he feels differently.

When the taxi with my parents pulls away, Dell and I stand there, a little shell-shocked.

"Should we find your mother before we go?" I ask.

He shakes his head. "We'll call them in the morning. We should go fetch Grace from Aunt Marge."

"You think your mom called her and told her what happened?" I ask. I picture Marge taking some terrible vengeance out on Grace.

"No. She doesn't have a phone and probably had to catch up on her work. It'll be okay. Besides, Marge is a sweet lady. And practical when it comes to Mom."

We walk to the rented white SUV. Bits of gravel crunch beneath my feet. I'm still not sure how to process the evening. So many things were said.

When Dell starts the car, I say, "We don't even know who knows what. Your mom didn't seem to really understand that Grace isn't mine. Neither of our dads heard the conversation. Mom is, God, I don't even know what Mom is thinking!"

He heads to the highway.

"I guess I knew this day was coming," he says.

"When everyone finds out about Grace?" I ask. My voice has a high, hysterical quality I don't like.

"I really think Grace is safe enough," he says. "Both our sets of parents realize they should leave her out of this."

"What about your name? Your past?" I stare out the side window. "Are you okay with everyone knowing who you are now? Blue collar and all?"

He doesn't answer. The lights blur past our window.

"Our parents knowing doesn't mean the world knows."

"If they can be discreet." None of them were being particularly calm. Mom has an Instagram following approaching half a million. One post and the world knows about Dell.

And whoa. I told my mother she ditched me. That she hadn't been there. I confronted her.

I feel lost. Confused. When do we bury our feelings and when do we let them out?

Dell reaches for my hand. "Let me take you somewhere before we pick up the baby," he says.

That's probably a good idea. We weren't even gone two hours. It's fine to slow down. Maybe I can compose myself before I face Marge. Hopefully Daniel Dean won't be around. I have a hard time staying straight-faced around him.

They're all so hard. All of Dell's family. What is it? Being southern? Poor?

We've driven several minutes before I figure it out. They say the truth. They don't hide it behind politeness or sugarcoat it. They don't therapy it out or pretend it doesn't exist.

They live out in the open. Say what they think. If people get mad, let 'em get mad.

They seem happy. As happy as any of us ever get.

I think of the party, the dancing, the pride they took in everything from their VA Hall to their roasted pig. It didn't take catered food or party planners or extravagance to be a good memory.

I could have done without the ball-and-chain shirt, though.

A smile flirts with my lips. I'm feeling better.

"Working it through?" Dell asks, his fingers clasped around mine.

"Maybe," I say. I kick off my shoes. I'm tired of this dress, tired of being looked at, examined, questioned. I just want to "be."

We pull up in a small parking lot nestled in trees.

"Where are we?" I ask.

"Vulcan Trail," he says. "Up there is one of the oldest parks in Birmingham, including the Vulcan, an iron statue."

We get out of the car. The statue is lit up, way above us on the hill. It's enormous, on a tall slender pillar.

"We can go see the statue if you like," he says.

"Maybe we can come back to it when Grace is older," I say.

"Good plan." Dell takes my hand and we walk along the trail in the dark. The moon and the spillover light from the park above provide enough light for us not to stumble.

There's no one here. We come to a clearer space, and all of Birmingham seems laid out below.

"It's lovely," I say.

Dell puts his arm around me. We look at the sight for a moment.

"Tough night," he says. "You doing okay?"

My voice sounds gritty. "Oh, I don't know. All our secrets got spilled and I told my mother how I felt about her leaving, and I have no idea what to do next."

He squeezes me tightly against him. "Everyone will think things over tonight. You know what I believe?"

I look up at him. He's ruggedly handsome in this

light. Strong and stalwart. "What?"

"That Grace will be the thing that brings us all together. We can't blow apart, let our families fragment. If we do, someone loses Grace."

"I guess this was exactly the time for this to happen. Weddings are happy events. Everyone will recover for that."

"Exactly," he says.

"I hope so." My mom is a tough nut. But then, so is his. "We can always elope."

"Exactly. They'll be afraid of that."

"After all, you have a private plane," I say with a laugh. "You showboat."

He chuckles. "That I am."

The night air is cool and I'm glad for Dell's warmth. I slide my hand beneath his sports coat. "It's lovely here. Quiet. Peaceful."

"It is," he says, and his voice has a husky quality to it, rumbling and low.

The sound of it wakes up parts of me. We're so close, our arms entwined. We've never had so much peace in the outdoors, not together. It can't be managed where we live. There's too much bustle, so much noise.

He turns me to him, and I melt against his body. He leans down, his lips brushing mine. The hard evening falls away as his mouth takes over, warm, seeking, insistent.

His hands move around my body, sliding along my waist. He caresses my back, my ribs.

The kiss deepens, our mouths seeking more. He tastes faintly of sweet liquor. I'm lost in him, lost in these woods, in the quiet.

His hands slide down my hips to the backs of my thighs. I feel aloft as he grips them, lifting me off the ground.

I tuck my legs around him, the skirt of my dress riding up.

And I feel him, hard against me, his body responding.

He takes a few steps forward, walking between a bench and a stone wall. The distance is perfect. My back presses into the stone, cushioned by my dress and my sweater. My feet reach the metal of the bench. I'm suspended, Dell between my legs, pressing me into the wall. His mouth moves to my neck, my collarbone.

His hands are more free, one cupping me,

holding me in place while the other reaches behind me for the zipper of the dress.

I cock my hips forward, giving him room between my back and the wall. This connects us more securely, his erection raging there, pressing into me through my skirt and panties.

The top of the dress goes loose, and now Dell tugs down the thin strap beneath my cardigan. The top falls enough to expose the lacy cup of my bra. He slides down that strap, tugging everything down on one side.

One rosy breast is revealed to the moonlight, the nipple tightening instantly in the cool air.

His head dips down, catching it in his mouth. It's warm and wet, and I suck in a breath.

He rocks against me where we join below. My hands clasp his shoulders, but I reach down, lifting my skirt out of the way.

His free hand moves down, beneath the dress, sliding up my thigh. He reaches my panties, small and delicate, and flirts with the lacy edge.

I push with my feet to create a little space between our bodies, flattening against the wall. I reach between us to unbutton his khakis, tugging the zipper.

His boxers are soft satin and easy to push out of the way. He springs up to me, and I slide my hand along his length. He groans, leaving my breast and burying his face in my neck. I work him a little longer, fingers tight, moving with his rhythm until I can feel the veins pulsing under his skin.

"Arianna," he says, both hands holding me now, lifting me higher. I let him go and hang on, arms trembling, anxious and needy.

His hand slides between my legs and shifts the panties aside. Fingers slip inside me, and I clutch his head, sucking in another breath.

He works my body, in and out, finding the sweet nub that aches for him, and circling it with his thumb.

The tension begins to increase and I rock with his movements. I want him now, here, right here. "Dell, please, yes," I say.

He withdraws his hand and shifts until his erection presses against me. He pulls the panties aside again, and then he's there, sliding inside, our bodies flush against each other.

I feel so full, so complete. He holds me in his hands, lifting me, then letting me fall on him, again and again.

I push against the bench, adding pressure and speed. My fingers grip his shoulders, bulging and strong.

He's so deep, so powerful. My need for him overwhelms me, flooding me with heat. The tightness around him builds, then pauses for a long golden moment, suspended, intense.

Then it all lets go.

I cry out, pulsing around him, my body exploding in a shower of pleasure and bright sparks. Dell grips me, holding me still, rocking inside, and I feel the warm rush of him spilling inside me.

We clutch each other, holding on, the breeze tickling my cheeks and teasing my hair. It's intoxicating, being outside, feeling so intense and loved and full.

Voices carry from above. We look up. We can't see anyone around the statue, which means they can't see us either. The figure of the giant man, arm outstretched, is a silhouette in the trees.

Dell withdraws and sets me down. We arrange our clothes.

"I bet you took all the girls here," I say.

He laughs. "No, no, I did not."

We hold hands as we walk back to the car. It's time to fetch our baby girl. Face more family. And see how the chips are going to fall from this very eventful night.

Chapter 25: Dell

I'm expecting the call that comes the next morning. We decided to stay in town another day to see if we could smooth over everything that happened the night before.

Arianna glances up from where she sits on the floor with Grace, trying to show her the proper hands-and-knees crawl. "Your mom?" she asks.

I nod and answer the call.

"Hey, Mom," I say.

"Hasmund Dell Brant McDonald, your brother just Googled you!" she says.

"Hey, you know Google," I answer.

"Don't get smart. Pack up that baby of yours and get your tail over here." Her voice is no-nonsense, no arguments allowed.

"All right. Should we bring something?"

"Yes. Lunch. Fancy lunch. The most expensive goddamn lunch in Birmingham."

Well, that's a switch. "Okay," I say. She hangs up and I shove the phone in my pocket.

"What's the damage?" Arianna asks.

"I'm to pick up the fanciest lunch to be procured in Birmingham and bring it with you and the baby to her house."

Arianna laughs. "Well, okay. What's the fanciest lunch in Birmingham?"

"Probably not something you can get for takeout," I say.

"I think this is exactly the sort of challenge Dell Brant excels at," she tells me. Her eyes are sparkling with mirth. I'm glad she's enjoying this.

I think for a moment, glancing at the clock. Just past ten on a Sunday. What is open? What is fancy? There should be brunches.

This is why I have assistants. But today, I will do my own legwork.

I start with the concierge at the hotel. He gives me some names to work with. The first one straight-out hangs up when I ask for a delivery.

That's a new feeling.

The second one assures me that very little on their menu will hold up to travel. "It's beauty on the plate," the man says. "But it will be tragic in a box."

Oookay.

"Maybe just go the bakery route," Arianna says. "I think your mom is just ribbing you about having so much money."

She's probably right. To cover my bases, I have two separate bakeries make deliveries to my mother's trailer, and I call on the driver I haven't used all weekend to pick up a variety of French cheeses, bread, and fruit from a tea shop and then a selection of sausages, breakfast ham, and steak from another restaurant.

"Don't forget drinks," Arianna says. "Unless you want another day of Tequila Sunrises."

I send a note to the driver to pick up a selection of juices and to stop by a Starbucks for a carton of fresh coffee.

"You think that will do it?" I ask Arianna as we

load up Grace's diaper bag.

"It will be fine," she says. "Even if they have Marge and Travis and Daniel Dean over, it will be enough."

"It will be enough for twenty people, I think," I say. But it pleases me to finally be able to do something for my family with style.

We wait for the driver to let us know he has arrived. I was tempted to change out the simple white SUV for something fancier now that the jig is up, as they say, but I don't.

Arianna makes no progress with Grace, who is determined to keep her army crawl. Finally, we get the call from downstairs that our car is waiting.

"Good morning, Mr. Brant," the driver says as he opens the back door. He looks very Alabaman, dressed in jeans and a denim shirt, gray hair and a beard. "I have all the items you requested."

"Thank you," I say, buckling Grace into her seat. There isn't room for the car seat and both Arianna and me in the back, so I slide in next to the baby and let Arianna take the front.

We're quiet as we head through town to the trailer park. Arianna fusses with her blouse, an earthy green explosion of ruffles that looks a good deal fancier than what she's worn so far. Perhaps she is done with the ruse as well, or else her mother's comments cut her.

"You look lovely," I say, leaning forward. "Though I like you best in skirts."

She blushes at that. "Thank you. I'm glad you don't feel you need the baseball cap anymore."

"Pointless," I say, and sit back. Birmingham rolls by, streets I once knew, some changed, some things the same. Like my family.

"Is this it, sir?" the driver asks uncertainly as we approach the entrance to the trailer park.

"Yes, third one down on the left," I say.

"Shall I wait here?" he asks.

I hesitate. In New York a driver always stays with the car, because generally there is nowhere to park anyway.

"What do you usually do?" I ask.

"Oh, I bring things to read," he says.

"You should come in," Arianna says. "We have all this food anyway."

I think the man will turn her down, as that would be a very odd thing to suggest in the circles we run in.

But he nods. "I was sure hoping one of those sausages would have my name on it."

"And now it does," she says. "What's your name?"

"Martin," he says. "Martin Jones."

"Well, Martin, help us take things inside and we'll find a place for you." Arianna opens her own door.

I pull Grace from her carrier. Martin opens my door on his way to the back of the SUV. I hand Grace to Arianna and go back to help him unload.

There are a lot of boxes and bags and containers.

"You expecting a lot of people?" he asks.

"Not too many," I say. "But very hungry people."

Martin laughs. "Can amount to the same thing."

We manage to arrange it all and follow Arianna up the steps. Martin hangs back a bit as she knocks on the door.

"Nice idea to invite him," I say to her.

"I figure we may need all the buffer we can get," she says.

We're still standing there, waiting on the door, when a gleaming black Lincoln Town Car also pulls up.

"I guess we can figure out who that is," I say.

"They invited my parents too?" Arianna's face is full of shock.

I turn to Martin. "This is about to get interesting," I say.

The driver of the Town Car jumps out and dashes around to open the back door. Bridget steps out, as elegant as ever in a taupe pencil skirt and silk blouse.

"Is that a cashmere wrap?" Arianna asks, her eyes narrowing. "Of course it is."

As Cambridge emerges from the car, the door to the trailer opens behind us.

"Good to see everybody's made it," Mom says. She steps back to let us in. "You brought a friend?"

"This is Martin," Arianna says, and gives no further explanation.

I have to hide my smile.

We pause to wait for the Harts to come up the steps. Bridget looks at the park with great interest. Cambridge places his hand on her back to move her toward the door.

Mom holds the screen open. I turn to the living room. Dad is sprawled on the sofa, a boot up on the coffee table. Mom must have made him dress up a little, as he has a button-down shirt on with his jeans. Her shirt seems new, a long-sleeved red number with little yellow flowers on it. It looks totally wrong on her.

Donovan sits in one of the kitchen chairs, leaning forward with his elbows braced on his knees. He's the most casual of all of us, just a T-shirt and sweatpants. He's not trying to make an impression, clearly.

Arianna sits on the love seat, jiggling Grace. I take my boxes and bags to the kitchen, and Martin follows. The Harts come in.

"Who are all these people?" Martin asks me quietly. "Everybody acts like it's a funeral."

"Future in-laws," I say.

"No kidding," he says. "I'll unpack so you can catch up."

I nod. Pink boxes from the bakeries are already stacked on the counter. Mom has sprung for the fancy paper plates today, the heavy-duty ones with blue flowers printed on them. As a kid we always got the thin ones with the curved edges. You could cut right through them with a butter knife.

When I step back toward the living room, Bridget and Cambridge are standing awkwardly by the TV.

"Well, come on in," Mom says. "Cambridge, park yourself next to your new best bud. Bridget, I imagine you want next to Arianna to get a gander at that baby."

Arianna gives her mother a small smile as Bridget navigates the coffee table to sit next to her. Grace spots the shiny bold necklace on Bridget's chest and lunges for it.

"Might want to take off those earrings if you hold her," Arianna says. "She'll jerk those right out."

Bridget nods, tugging the big gold pieces from her ears and depositing them into her purse. Now that she's close, she can't take her eyes off Grace.

I know I should move forward to shake Cambridge's hand, at least. But that will put me next to my father. And I'm not interested in doing that. I sit in a chair next to Donovan and lean in.

"So what's our mother got planned here?" I ask.

He shrugs. "She just dragged me out of bed five minutes ago. I had no idea she was bringing everybody." He smooths his wild hair self-consciously.

"Late night?" I ask.

He grins. "Remember that girl in black who took

us to the Sky Box?"

I nod.

"I think I'm in love."

I elbow him. "Aren't you going back to Texas tomorrow?"

He frowns. "Yeah."

"We have some food in the kitchen," Mom announces. "I made sure Hasmund — Dell — brought things that you all would like." She gestures at the Harts. "I figure he'd know those things better than me."

Dad stands up. "I'm not shy," he says. "Come on, Cam."

"I'm fine for the moment," Bridget says. "Let me see this child." She reaches for Grace and Arianna tentatively shifts her over to her mother's lap.

"Come fetch some food," Dad says to us boys, coming up behind Martin. "I'm Byron," he says, shaking the man's hand. "Have I seen you around?"

"I work for Carter's Limousine Service," Martin says. "Been driving folks around since I retired from offshore work."

Dad snaps his fingers. "You must be a friend of Aaron Redding. He used to drive for Carter."

"I remember Aaron."

The three of them load up plates and take them to the table. It's still set up for six. Donovan and I toss some meat and rolls on our plates and join them.

The women stay in the living room, fussing over the baby.

There's something very familiar about the setup. Men eating and women tending to the kids. It's how I grew up.

Arianna looks over at us and nods at me. I can see she's relieved things are easy right now.

It's Martin who keeps the conversation going. "I hear there's going to be a wedding," he says.

"My boy here is marrying that gal over there," Dad says, pointing her out. "That's their kid."

"Cute little bugger," Martin says. "You all met before?"

"Last night," Cambridge answers. "We were up at the greyhound races."

"I haven't watched the dogs race in years," Martin says. "You win any?"

"Betting is for fools with too much money," Dad says. "Though I guess my boy here can spare it." He squints at me. "I hear you have your own plane."

I tear the end off a croissant. "I do."

Dad shoves Donovan on the shoulder. "When you going to get a plane, Donny boy?"

Donovan shakes his head. "Let me have my first day on the job, then we'll talk."

Everything is oddly easy. Donovan talks about the company he's going to work for. Cambridge gives him advice about benefits.

This isn't going badly at all.

But then Mom stands up. "I think we ought to start planning a wedding right here in Birmingham."

Arianna's mouth falls open.

And Bridget says, "Over my dead body."

Chapter 26: Arianna

"I'm not familiar with Birmingham," I say, feeling frantic. I glance over at Dell. He's giving me a pained look.

"I cannot imagine there is anyplace suitable," Mom says.

I elbow her. What has happened to her manners?

She bounces Grace and ignores me.

"Now, there's that uppity attitude again," Wynona says. "Same one that was all over the racetrack last night. You don't think there's pretty weddings here in Alabama?"

Mom looks around, as if realizing she's offended

everyone. "Arianna is my only child, and I want the best for her."

Dell stands up at that and comes close, sitting on the arm of the love seat next to me. "Mom, I believe it's the bride's decision on planning the wedding. You and I are in charge of the rehearsal dinner."

Wynona's mouth is a tight line. "If they are in charge, they'll have it someplace like Paris, France, or, I don't know, some fancy-pants museum. I can't go to that. Your father won't go. Think of YOUR family."

She has a point. Marge and Travis would be excluded if it's far. And Dell's grandma Jessie can't travel easily.

I have to speak up at this. "I hate that the wedding is already causing us to fight. We'll figure something out."

"The wedding is not the problem," Wynona says. "It's that you two didn't trust any of us with anything about your lives. This baby is eight months old and we didn't even know she existed until this weekend."

Now the whole room is with her. Mom, Dad, Byron. Even Martin looks a little stricken.

"It's complicated," Dell ventures, but his mother cuts him off.

"Nonsense. It's a baby, not a rocket ship." Wynona stands against the wall between the living room and the dining table, arms crossed over her chest. "How many people know you are Dell Brant?"

Dell frowns. "Thousands. Ten thousand. I don't know. I sometimes make the news."

"And how many know you are Hasmund McDonald?"

"Just family. People at the racetrack. A few at college."

Wynona jabs her finger at him. "The people you were embarrassed to know."

I can't stand this any longer. "You know, Dell and I are trying to make this right," I say. "That's why we're here. But if you can't sit and listen to US, then we have to go."

I stand up and lean down to take the baby from my mother. "We can elope. Forget all this drama. It's our day, and we won't have any of you all ruining it."

Mom doesn't want to let go of Grace. "Sit down, Arianna. Explain it to us, if you can."

I don't sit. I stand in front of all of them, Mom and Grace on the love seat next to Dell, the other men at the table.

"Grace's biological mother turned her over to Dell just a few months ago. It took us time to figure out what we were going to do. Until we were sure Grace could be ours, we kept it to ourselves."

"Who is this woman?" Wynona asks. "Who would abandon their own baby?"

"She's not able to care for her," I say. "She left her for the baby's sake."

Mom speaks up. "I am quite sure Dell and Arianna are perfectly capable of taking care of the legal issues. We just aren't sure about all the secrecy."

"We have to ask you to help us on that," Dell says. "For Grace. It's her life. We want it to be as normal for her as possible."

That gets them. Everyone looks at Grace, calmly sitting on my mother's lap, a gummy teething ring jabbed in her mouth. She seems to realize she's the center of attention, because she holds the ring in the air, both arms out, and jabbers as if she's making a great speech.

"It's the kids that matter," Wynona says, and everyone seems to be back on the same page. "Your secret is safe with us. All of us in this room, right?"

Everyone murmurs.

Martin says, "I didn't hear a thing."

We've forgotten a perfect stranger is in the room. "Thank you, Martin," I say.

He gets up. "I'll get the ladies some food," he says, heading for the kitchen. "Sounds like you all have some planning to do."

Wynona sits on the sofa and pats the cushion. "Come here, child," she says. "What sort of wedding do you want?"

I'm not really sure. But I look around at all of them, my elegant parents and Dell's very different family, even Martin, who represents the regular Alabaman.

And I think I might be getting an idea.

Epilogue: The Wedding: Arianna

Six months later

No one expected the wind.

Marge stands behind Wynona, rapidly braiding her hair and setting it with a metric ton of hair spray. "Hand me a pin, sis," she says.

Wynona passes her one, holding it over her shoulder.

The stylist attending to my hairdo adds another row of pearl seed clips to one side. "I'm doubling up," she says. "Your hair isn't going to move even if a hurricane hits."

"Don't mention any natural disasters," Mom says. "Not when we're out at sea." She has two stylists working on her, one on hair, one on makeup. We have a ridiculous amount of help. Even Grace has her own assistant.

I scrunch my face at the baby, now fourteen months and toddling pretty well. She makes the same face back at me.

She's precious in a ruffly white dress. It has a long white cape that hits the back of her knees, tied to her shoulders with little pink bows. She's like a mini super hero.

She holds a basket, although she can't really walk and carry it at the same time without help. She's not that steady.

"I love the cape," Wynona says. "It's a hoot."

"What are you talking about?" Mom asks. She doesn't think anything wedding related should be a "hoot."

Dell's mom and I pass a conspiratorial glance. I guess nobody told Mom about Grace's cape.

I'm certainly not going to enlighten her.

"Your hair looks great," I say. "Elegant and windproof."

"We could move the wedding indoors, you know," she says.

"Now, Bridget," Wynona scolds her. "Arianna wanted a wedding on the sea. It's not the same in a ballroom."

"We're all going to blow away," Mom says.

"Nonsense," Wynona fires back.

They've been at each other like this since we picked Wynona and Byron up in Birmingham, but there's no real malice in their bickering. Just two very different women working out their vastly opposite worldviews.

A lot like Dell and his father. They've never made up, not really. But Dell did take Byron on his plane. With my dad there to referee, they managed to find some common ground. They can be civil, if nothing else.

So it's not perfect, but it's pretty good. Good enough.

Marge backs away from Wynona. "You're as pretty as a picture," she says.

Wynona touches her hair. "It feels like a football

on my head."

"It's lovely," I say. And it is. Marge has worked the braids together into a French twist. Neither of them were willing to let one of our stylists touch them.

"All done here." My hairdresser pats my shoulder. I stand up. The white silk robe floats around me. My makeup is done. It's probably about time to put on my dress.

The photographer hurries in. "Got the groom and the groomsmen," he says. "Time for some preparation photos of the bridal party."

"Great," Wynona says flatly. "I don't have my face on."

Mom stares the photographer down. "You will not take a single image of me until I say so." One of her girls holds a white towel in front of her face.

"Well, we agree on that," Wynona says. She and Marge look at each other and crack up.

"How about the bride?" he asks. "Can we get some of you?"

"Of course," I say. I pick up Grace and hold her up to my cheek.

"Beautiful," he says, snapping shot after shot.

Grace lets go of the basket and it hits the ground, petals scattering. She lets out an unhappy cry.

"It's okay, sugar lump," I say, setting her down. "You can put all the pretty petals back in the basket." Her baby cape almost flips over, revealing the words, but I quickly drop it back into place.

"Why don't you take Grace over to Dell?" I say to the girl who is watching her for the duration of the trip.

"Good idea," Marge says.

"In my day, babies were women's work," Mom says.

I have to laugh. "Mom, you had a nanny, a tutor, and a housekeeper watching over me."

"All women!" she says from behind the towel.

The photographer snaps shots of my dress, hanging by a window. We're on the upper level of the cruise ship in a triple suite, so there are balconies in every room.

When Dell and I settled on a cruise, we knew setting sail out of Mobile, Alabama, would satisfy both camps. Fancy and elite enough for the Harts. Close enough for the Birmingham contingent to drive up and get on the boat.

About four hundred of the ship's six hundred passengers are attending the wedding. My mother and father won the battle of large and inclusive over small and intimate. We had tried to book a private ship, but the size of our guest list made that impossible unless we waited two years for the wedding.

That wasn't going to happen.

"Let me get snaps of the ring," the photographer says. His assistant brings him my flower bouquet, and he takes several shots of my hand with the arrangement, the diamond Dell bought in Paris almost a year ago bright and sparkling.

My mother finally decides she is "done enough" for photographs, and we take a few shots together with me still in the robe. Then I get partially dressed and we take more of her pretending to fasten the back of the gown.

I grow more jittery as the moment arrives. I'm not sure why.

My mom is doing fine. Dell's dad has controlled himself. Wynona is our comic relief.

We have plenty of help, assistants and stylists and more than one butler. After an argument, our butler Bernard was convinced to go mostly off duty. He did insist that no one but him would assist Dell in the preparation for the actual wedding.

Dell assigned a butler to his butler just for fun. Every time we have seen the two men together, they have been arguing over the correct fold for a silk handkerchief or the proper way to store a decanter of brandy.

It's been amusing.

Finally, the dress is secured, by a stylist, not my mother, and the photographers leave to prepare for the ceremony itself. The entire main deck has been cleared and set with rows and rows of white chairs.

"Fifteen minutes!" Cara, the wedding planner, pokes her head in. "I assume everyone is ready!"

"We are!" Mom says.

"Time for us to go too," Marge says. She hustles Wynona out.

The stylists give me and Mom one more look over and assure us they'll be on standby if the weather plays havoc with our dresses or hair. Then they also abandon the room.

Mom gives me one more kiss. "You have a lovely moment up there. I am so very honored and pleased to be here with you on this day."

This makes my eyes tear up.

So many times she wasn't there.

But today, she's here.

"Don't you cry," she says, dabbing the corners of my eyes with a small tissue. "You paid very good money for this look. And it's lovely."

I try to smile. "I'm glad you're here, Mom."

"Of course I would be. And I know I wasn't always. I know I put my work before you. I knew it at the time." She tucks the tissue in her sleeve. "I just didn't know how to stop. I didn't know how to just sit with a small child and *be*."

Now her eyes are wet.

"Don't you cry either," I say.

She nods, pulling the tissue out again. "I'm glad you've made better decisions with your daughter, even you've attended woefully few charity balls."

There's a knock at the door. Dad pops his head in. "Is it time for me to escort my baby girl down the aisle?"

"It is," I say.

Donovan is behind him, followed by Taylor. She brings in Grace. "Time for us to get ready for our big moment!" she says.

Donovan takes Mom's arm. Since I don't have a brother, and Dad will be with me, Donovan's escorting her to her seat before heading back to walk in with Dell as best man.

"Look at you," Dad says. "You are a vision."

"Super beautiful," Taylor says. She holds Grace on her hip. Grace keeps tipping the basket, spilling petals.

The other bridesmaids flow into the room. "It's almost time!" one says, a daughter of one of my father's associates. Three of them are girls I barely know, part of the package agreement with my parents.

Then there are some of the teachers at my Child Spa. I brought as many as I could spare for a few days. Mom insisted I had to have at least seven to have a respectable showing of support for a wedding this size.

I allowed it. It didn't matter to me who stood up there as long as I was next to Dell.

Dell could not be convinced to place his dad next to him, so it's his brother, his uncle Travis, Daniel Dean, and four men from his company. We wanted Bernard to take part, but he said he would have plenty of duties already.

The wedding planner returns. "Everyone is seated," she says. "Ready?"

I give a nod.

The bridesmaids follow her, my father and I in the rear. The girl helping Grace takes her from Taylor.

Their dresses are all the palest possible shade of pink, sleek sheaths that flare out behind them on the floor. They look like a row of tulips walking down the hall.

I press a hand to my belly where the beaded bodice meets the flare of the skirt. This body couldn't do a mermaid dress, but the empire waist is flattering and lovely. The train is a mile long, dissolving into gentle tiers of sheer tulle and seed pearls.

I realize I've forgotten my flowers, but Taylor turns when I stop. She's holding both of our bouquets. "That's what I'm here for," she says. "Don't worry."

"Thank you," I tell her. "I guess I need you as much at my wedding as at my spa."

My father takes my arm. "It will be fine, Arianna. Everything is well in hand."

We approach the side exit to the side of the boat that will lead us to the main deck. When the wedding planner slides the door open, I breathe in the sea air, salty and warm.

I feel better instantly. We walk along the side deck, past a few guests playing shuffleboard on the polished wood. They stop to watch us go by.

We pause at the end of the wall. The music greets us, a full orchestra playing near the stern of the deck. The white chairs are filled with guests. A white gazebo, constructed just for our wedding, is covered with white flowers at the apex of the ship. The minister waits beneath it in a white robe, his arms cradling a black binder.

As we wait, Dell appears on the opposite side, coming from the other side deck. He has always worn a suit well, and his tuxedo is no exception, black and formal with a bright white shirt and white tie. He looks spectacular. I can scarcely believe he is about to be my husband.

Behind him, of course, is Maximillion, our greyhound, resplendent with his shiny pale fur and dashing black bow tie. When Dell stops, Maximillion immediately sits very properly on his haunches, his nose in the air. The crowd laughs.

Donovan is next. When he stands beside Dell, he

ribs him about something, and they all chuckle. Maximillion turns as if to tell them, "Be proper, now."

A Birmingham cousin approaches us, a young woman in a peach dress, her hair blowing every direction. She holds the hand of a small boy, about three. He's Trey, the ring bearer. She must be Amanda.

I have only heard of them. She's the daughter of one of Byron's sisters. She lives in Atlanta, so I hadn't gotten around to meeting her yet.

"This is Trey," she says. "I hope he does what he's supposed to!"

The assistant sets Grace down next to him. They stare at each other for a moment. Grace gives him her serious expression.

I kneel down next to them. "Hello, Trey, this is Grace. Do you think you can walk with her down the aisle? She has only just learned to walk."

The boy looks up at his mother, who nods at him.

He takes Grace's hand.

"Okay," Amanda says. "Cross your fingers."

"It's time," the planner says. "Just wait on the music change."

We listen for a moment. The song ends and there is a small pause. I spot Grandma Jessie on the end of the row, ribbons threaded through the spokes of her wheelchair.

Everyone is here.

The first bridesmaids make their way to the center aisle and begin their slow walk to the front.

Taylor hands me my bouquet. "You ready for this?"

"I think so," I say.

"Not too late to jump ship and row back to shore," Dad says.

I laugh. "We're two days out to sea now."

"That would be a fair bit of paddling."

"My turn," Taylor says. She kisses my cheek. "I would never have seen this day coming based on the moment you two met."

I have to agree. Dell was an arrogant, stiff, womanizing bachelor.

But I hadn't been the one to change him.

She had.

Grace.

Taylor departs. Amanda and the assistant help the two little ones to the end of the aisle.

"Now, go!" Amanda says.

The assistant hangs back, not sure if she should follow. They toddle forward. Grace drops her basket, and Trey picks it up and hands it back to her.

The crowd makes a collective happy sigh.

"Let's get in place," the planner says.

My father and I move to the end of the aisle. All eyes are on the little ones, still making their way to the front.

Dad and I shift into position and the planner moves behind me to straighten my train.

Grace and Trey keep moving forward at their toddling pace. Then Grace sees Dell and calls out, "Dada!" and races toward him.

My eyes spring with tears again, and I wish for Mom's tissue.

Dell picks Grace up and kisses her cheek. *Dada* had been her first word. She's still working on *Mama*.

"Here, sweetheart," my own father says, passing me a tissue. "Your mother told me to be prepared."

I dab my eyes and tuck the tissue into the bottom of the bouquet. "Thank you."

"Looks like that little girl has her daddy wrapped around her finger," he says.

"She does."

Taylor comes forward to take Grace from Dell. She protests until she sees Wynona, and toddles over to her. Wynona picks her up and sits her in her lap on the front row.

The music shifts again and the minister lifts his hands for everyone to stand.

My father moves us forward, and I feel all eyes shifting to me.

I keep my gaze on Dell. He stands tall, his hands clasped together. He can't take his eyes off me, nor me him.

Calm, immutable Dell. It's his last moments as a single dad. We've been in this together for a long while now, but this seals it. I will be his. He will be mine. And Grace will have her family come together, months after her adoption made us officially her parents.

We walk past people I recognize and others I don't know. Faces, lives, other love affairs, more families.

I keep my attention on Dell, this moment, this incredible beautiful anticipation. As I make it to the front of the chairs, the sky opens wide, blue and clear, separated from the ocean by only the most subtle shift of color.

When I reach Dell, my father passes my hand to him. Dell kisses my fingers.

"Take care of her," my father says.

"You know I will," Dell replies.

And then it's just the two of us, repeating the words we practiced, adding a few of our own. The music plays. The unity candle blows out and we have to light it three times, laughing all the while.

When the minister is about to pronounce us husband and wife, Grace decides she has had enough. She wiggles down from Wynona's lap and races forward, crashing into Dell's legs.

He laughs and picks her up.

The minister nods at us. "I guess I will simply have to pronounce you a family," he says.

I kiss Grace on the tippy top of her soft downy head, just now gathering enough wisps of hair to hold a tiny bow. Dell does the same.

Then we hold her between us, our lips finding that place that has long since become familiar, our bodies creating an arc over Grace. It's as it should be, as she brought us together. Her needs superseded ours. And in loving her, we learned to love each other as well.

When we finally part, the crowd cheers and claps. Dell picks up Grace, lifting her high in the air.

As he brings her down, he flips her little white cape to the opposite side.

Everyone erupts as they spot the words printed on it.

I'm the Plus One.

Also by JJ Knight

The UNCAGED LOVE Series
The FIGHT FOR HER Series

www.jjknight.com

Made in the USA
Monee, IL
08 February 2024

53161296R00142